PRAISE FOR J.S. ARQUIN

★ ★ ★ ★ ★ "Divergent meets Hunger Games and then some. Could not put this one down."

★ ★ ★ ★ ★ "Writer in control of all. The story sweeps you along with it."

★ ★ ★ ★ ★ "Absolutely loved this book!"

★ ★ ★ ★ ★ "This is book one of a series I just can't wait to read more of."

★ ★ ★ ★ ★ "The book is nonstop action and adventure."

★ ★ ★ ★ ★ "Found this gem. A great read. Solid sci-fi. Looking forward to more by this author."

★ ★ ★ ★ ★ "Like the Hunger Games, but better. I loved this book."

— - AMAZON REVIEWS OF ASCENT

Join J.S. Arquin's reader group for exclusive news and deals:
www.arquinworlds.com

SLIDE

BOOK TWO OF THE CRIMSON DUST CYCLE

J.S. ARQUIN

WORDS ON THE WIND LLC

Edited by C.B. Moore

Cover design: Covers by Christian

Paperback ISBN: 978-1-951968-04-5

Ebook ISBN: 978-1-951968-05-2

❁ Created with Vellum

For my mom, who always believed I should be a writer.

1

———

L ife never works out the way you plan. If someone had told me I'd fight my way out of the mines to become a Guardian only to spend more time crawling around in the mines, I'd have laughed in their face. Yet here I am in the dark, fifty meters below the surface, trying not to get my head cut off by a Horror.

I joined the Guardians to find my sister, Ianna. I fought my way up through the Guardian tournament so I'd have the power to find her. I had to do terrible things to survive, including maiming and killing other kids. But I did it. Me and my crew won the tournament. Against all odds, a bunch of rockheads became Guardians.

Now it's been months since that day, and three and a half years since Ianna was taken away from me. I've got a warpknife, silver armor, boosted strength and reflexes, and an AI co-pilot in my head. I've become a hero or a monster, depending on your point of view. And I'm still no closer to finding my sister.

I thought becoming a Guardian would give me the power to do anything. Make things better. Instead, I'm nothing but a grunt following orders. Crawling through the dark with my crew, patrolling the same dusting mines I worked so hard to win my way out of. Someone, somewhere, is laughing at me.

We've tracked a rogue Rock Horror to this abandoned mine outside the perimeter. It's been terrorizing the supply trains, carrying people off in the night, destroying trade goods, that sort of thing.

Horror activity has been on the upswing lately. No one knows why. Maybe it's mating season. Maybe they're bored and attacking human settlements is their idea of a good time.

The bottom line is new Guardians get sent out to solve the problems no one else wants to deal with. Which leads to me crawling through darkness, fifty meters underground, trying to avoid getting my head sliced off by a crystalline pincer the length of my leg.

"Any signs of life, Jmini?"

"That's a big negative, Capitan," my AI replies cheerfully, his old-fashioned British tones as out of place as ever. "This place is as lively as an officer's barracks at sunrise."

"Thanks for that lovely image, Jmini. As if Horrors creeping through my head in the dark weren't bad enough, now I've got hungover officers with bloodshot eyes and morning breath that would wake the dead."

"Always happy to help."

Jmini's sarcasm makes me smile. He's been watching my back ever since I salvaged him from the scrap heaps back when I was a dirty street kid. When Instructor Castle took him away from me during the final contest of the Guardian Tournament, I was afraid I'd lost him forever. I was over the moons when Shadow helped me get him back after graduation.

"Maro, you done farting around down there yet?" A bored, raspy voice crackles down the comm from the surface. "I'd like to be done before happy hour."

"Doing my best, sir." I grimace at my legal name. My parents may have named me Theo Maro, but only spine-straight officers use it. Everyone else calls me Twist. "No sign of our little friend yet."

Sergeant Dekin is a drunk with a gambling problem. Only the dregs get assigned to his squad, the grunts no one else wants. Which means jumped-up rockheads like me.

There's a sound in the darkness, somewhere off to my left. I freeze, listening, my augmented senses switching to high alert. The last thing you want is for a Horror to catch you by surprise.

Sweat trickles down the side of my neck, and I scratch at the greicagin shard embedded in my collarbone. The skin around it has been red and inflamed for months. I'm starting to think the incision is never going to heal completely.

The shard powers all the enhancements the Guardians have inserted into my body: boosted strength and reflexes, high-tech sight and hearing, an extra adrenaline gland and beefed-up heart and lungs.

Most of the time I don't feel any different, but when I activate all my augments at once I feel like a turbo-boosted HAMR droid. It's weird and frightening and awesome all at once. When you get right down to it, I'm powered the same way my warpknife is now. Maybe I've become a warpknife myself.

The color of the world shifts as Jmini adds infrared to my night vision.

"Thanks, Jmini. I didn't even have to ask."

"I live to anticipate your every whim, master."

The biggest drawback to my new systems is that I need an onboard AI to control them, which means Jmini now lives in a tiny implant behind my left ear. They say that eventually my body will figure out how to control the augments, but there's no timetable for how long that will take. Some Guardians master their implants in months, some take years. It's like learning to walk. It takes as long as it takes.

I like Jmini a lot, don't get me wrong. It's just weird having him with me 24/7. Sometimes a guy wants to poop in peace, you know?

My scanner says there's movement around the next bend. I press myself against the cold stone wall, my warpknife gripped in my right hand, the weight familiar and comforting. A faint green glow outlines the blade, the embedded power of its greicagin shard flowing up from the hilt.

"Shadow, are you reading this?"

"I see it, Twist."

Of course she sees it. Shadow is one of the best covert spies in Canyon City. She sees everything. But if push comes to shove, her thin cloaking armor and small frame are not what you want on the front line.

"Knott, are you close?"

"About a hundred meters away."

Spines. A hundred meters is a long way down here. It's not like a hundred meters on the surface. There's no straight-line travel underground. It's all fissures and cracks that have been expanded by generations of miners zig-zagging through the belly of the mountains according to the unpredictable whims of the griecagin strikes. If the conditions are challenging, a hundred meters down here could take ten minutes to traverse. Not good.

Knott's voice crackles again.

"Sit tight. I'll be there as soon as I can."

Sound advice. Knott's the designated tank of our crew, and her heavy-duty armor's about three times the size of mine. So if there's something nasty nearby, waiting for her to go in first is the right strategy.

Still, my skin is tingling, so I extend a little camera from my armor and periscope it around the corner. My eyes blur as my vision adjusts, and I have to blink a few times to focus. I'm still not used to having tech embedded in my skull. When I was a kid dreaming of being a Guardian with super-human abilities, it never occurred to me there might be drawbacks. Like having the mad desire to scratch the inside of your eyeball. I blink a few more times and do my best to ignore it.

With the infrared, I see them. Little things crawling over the walls of the cavern. There must be hundreds of them.

"What are those things, Jmini? Plakbeetles? Boneworms? I can't tell."

"They appear to resemble millipedes. Long, tubular bodies with many legs on each side."

"What do you mean, 'appear to resemble'? Are you telling me you don't know what they are?"

"Not with any degree of certainty, no. There are only about a thousand identified species on Greica, while the estimates of unidentified species run into the hundreds of thousands at least. There's a lot here we don't know."

"And don't care to know," Shadow adds.

"Well, there are more important things to focus on," Jmini huffs.

"Like where our Rock Horror is hiding." Knott steps into the cavern through another entrance, her bulk blazing like a star on my infrared.

"Twist, come take a look at this." Shadow's voice is quietly urgent.

I find her at the end of a side passage that curves away from the main chamber. She's standing in a tunnel that stretches away into darkness in both directions. But that's not why she called me over.

Off to one side of the tunnel a hole has been dug in the ground. It's full of turds. Human turds.

"A latrine?"

Shadow nods. "Used pretty recently too."

"What would people be doing down here?" I shine my light up and down the tunnel. Dusty tracks lead off into the darkness.

"Going places, it seems."

"Where would they be going? We're two kilometers outside the perimeter."

But I know the answer. The Outsiders must use this tunnel. My father's band of rebels, moving beneath the surface to avoid detection as they work to bring down the IEC.

I've got to warn them. Let them know this route has been compromised.

Then Shadow raises a grimmer possibility: "It could be slavers, smuggling people out of Canyon City. I've heard they sell them to the other colonies."

My blood runs cold as I track the possible outcomes. In the months since graduation, I've spent all my free time trying to track down Ianna. Without success. What if she was sold as a slave?

Canyon City is just one of the Five Canyons settlements. There are four other colonies out there in the scablands, but they're all at least two days away. If Ianna's been smuggled to one of them, finding her will be almost impossible.

Slaves. My lip curls in disgust. Just when you think Canyon City can't get any worse, someone has to go and start slaving.

I switch my comm over to our private channel.

"Let's keep this out of the report, OK?"

Shadow raises an eyebrow at me, but before she can respond the subterranean silence is pierced by the shriek of an angry Rock Horror.

2

Knott grapples with the Rock Horror, her hands locked around the base of its razor-sharp pincers. Her power armor whines with the strain of holding them at bay. The Horror's multi-faceted eyes gleam, iridescent above its yellow and blue carapace.

The Rock Horror is a small one, only about the size of a gravbike, which makes it close to an even match for Knott. They push back and forth, the Horror scuttling with its six short legs, Knott heaving with her two long ones. If Knott lets go of those pincers, they'll shred her armor like rice paper.

Of course, Knott is one of the strongest humans I've ever come across. Even with my augments, that Horror would probably tear me apart in seconds.

They're whirling around, jerking back and forth in unpredictable lurches. Shadow and I stand frozen, mesmerized by the struggle.

"Quit watching and help!" Knott growls, breaking us out of our stasis.

I draw my warpknife and step to the left.

"Turn on the juice, Jmini."

I shudder as my augments kick into battle mode. Adrenaline

pumps into my body. My heart hammers in my chest. Air whooshes into my lungs. I am stronger, faster, and hyper alert. The power of the greicagin shard tingles through my nerves like a thousand ants marching.

Shadow mirrors me, flanking the fighters. I try to time the Horror's thrashing, but just as I start to lunge in, its tail lashes out. There's a stutter in my reaction, a result of my body being not quite synced up with my augments yet, and the tail catches me on the wrist, sending my warpknife skittering across the floor.

"Spines!" I dive after it.

I'm down on my hands and knees in the dust when an awful shriek spikes into my skull. The pain takes my breath away. I collapse into a ball, clutching my head with both hands. The Rock Horror's emotions press down on me, the heavy despair of a mother whose child has been ripped from her grasp. It feels like the weight of a mountain. My eyes fill with tears. I can't move. I can hardly breathe. I'm choking on pain and sadness.

I don't know how long I lie there. It feels like hours.

Knott and Shadow finally manage to finish the monster off without me. As the Horror's massive heart pumps its last, the weight of the despair lifts. I scrub my hands over my face, drawing in a shaky breath. Those things definitely do not go down quietly.

"Good thing I distracted it for you."

Shadow rolls her eyes.

"Are you done picking your noses down there?" Dekin breaks in. "Happy hour started fifteen minutes ago. I'm docking you all two credits for every minute I miss."

"What do you want us to do with the carcass?" Shadow asks.

"Stuff it and mount it beside your bed. I don't give two spines what you do with it."

We all look at each other.

"Maybe they will take care of it." Knott points with her chin. The pseudo-millipedes are making a beeline for the corpse. There are dozens of them, with more converging from across the chamber. They gather in thick columns, legs moving in waves, brown sausage bodies nosing blindly. When they reach the Horror's body, they start to eat their way inside.

I take a step back. "Creepy."

Shadow shudders. "Let's get out of here."

I take one last look at the latrine before I go, my eyes following the footprints stretching away into the darkness. Were some of them left by my sister? If there are slavers in Canyon City, I've got to find out who they are.

By the time we get back to the Mesa, the comedown from my adrenaline boost has left me unsteady and ravenous. I scarf down a protein bar as I strip off my sweaty armor, then sit in front of my locker and chew, trying to figure out my next step.

My search for Ianna has been leading me into dead ends all over Canyon City. Now that I know there are slavers operating in the Five Canyons, I'm afraid she might not be in Canyon City at all. That could make finding her nearly impossible.

I trace the pendant at the base of my throat: three copper circles inside a metal crescent, representing my family. It was made by my dad years ago, before he died in an Outsider bombing attack. Except he's not dead. He faked his death to become an Outsider, hiding in the scabland cave systems beyond the perimeter.

My dad opened my eyes to the way the IEC has been exploiting the people of Canyon City for generations. He showed me how our grandparents' debt we've been working off is just a carrot they dangle to keep us working, so they can keep getting richer. That debt is never going away. The only way Canyon City will ever be free is to get rid of the IEC.

My dad and Tempest, the leader of the Outsiders, turned me into a double agent and sent me back into Merrimac to complete my training. Now I'm an Outsider mole. I'm pretending to be a Guardian, but really I'm just waiting for the signal from the Outsiders. Waiting until it's time to bring everything crashing down.

I wonder if my dad would know anything about the slavers. They have to be moving through the Outsider's territory. I need to get him a message; he'd want to find Ianna as badly as I do.

Except that the Outsiders said they'd get in touch with me when the time was right. I don't know how to get a message to them. But I have an old friend who might.

Shadow nudges me with her elbow. Her kinky hair sticks out in little twists around her ebony face. "Are you coming to the parade?"

"What?"

"It's Founder's Day, remember?"

"Oh, right. I'll meet you there. I've got something I need to do first."

She smirks. "Does this 'something' have to do with that fancy new scarf you're wearing?"

Heat rises to my cheeks as I finger the scarf. It's a present from Kass, sky blue with black scrollwork along the edges. So soft you want to lie down and sink into it forever. A year ago I didn't know fabric this fine existed.

I thought Kass would disappear once we graduated from Merrimac. Leave our little student fling behind. Especially since my crew beat hers in our final exam. But here we are, months later, and somehow she's still coming down to see me a couple of times a week. I don't know what she sees in a rockhead like me, but I'm not going to poke the soap bubble too hard.

"No. It's something else."

"Oooo, something else. Does Kass know you're cheating on her?"

I choke. "I'm not cheating on her!"

Shadow laughs. "Don't be so serious, Twist. I'm just giving you the spines. Knott, are you coming?"

The big girl shakes her head, straight black hair waving over her forehead. "Sami is sick. I will take care of him."

"That's your brother?"

"Yes."

"But not the one who's having a baby with the silversmith girl."

"No."

"Spines, how many brothers do you have, Knott?" I ask.

A broad smile splits her wide, flat face. "Seven."

"Seven brothers? That's some biblical guano right there."

"A big family is the best thing. I am blessed to have family."

My smile is wistful. "I'm not going to argue with you there. One of these days I'm going to bring my family back together too."

Her dark eyes hold mine. "I will help any way I can, Twist. We are crew. Crew are family."

3

The crowds are already lining the dusty avenues between the spires of Canyon City, early arrivals claiming the best places. They've got picnic baskets, folding chairs, and parasols. Dirty kids chase each other across the street, laughing. Some of them swing sticks, playing at warpknives. Above, people lean out of open windows, waving down at friends and relatives.

The city rising around me is hollowed from the rock of the planet. Homes and buildings excavated directly from the forest of thick spires that rise at this end of a wide canyon. Like an enormous cluster of anthills or hives. The streets wind haphazardly between the spires; narrow, dusty tracts beaten hard and flat by generations of feet.

The dust gets into everything. Crimson dust that gathers in the folds in your clothes, cakes the corners of your mouth and eyes. It's like living in powdered blood.

A pang of nostalgia goes through me. I was one of those dirty kids, once upon a time. My sister, Ianna, loved the Founder's Day parade; she always made sure we staked out a good spot early.

My last happy memory of my family being all together was a morning just like this one.

Dad gave Ianna and me the pendants with the three copper circles as we sat waiting for the parade. If I'd known about the bomb that would blow our family apart a few days after that, would I have done anything differently? Been a better son? A better brother?

A better brother, certainly. If I could go back and do it again, I'd never let them separate us after Dad disappeared. I'd keep Ianna with me no matter what.

Guardians stand at the intersections in threes and fours, keeping watch over the festive crowd. Silver armor shines in the sunlight. They stand out from the tired, dusty rockheads like beings from another world.

Their armor gleams, but the Guardians' eyes are sharp, and their cannons are held ready. A short woman I don't recognize barks at some children whose stick fight has taken them too close to her corner. A little boy bursts into tears. His mother scoops him up and bustles away into the crowd. Passers-by bend their paths around the Guardian cluster.

I feel for the kid. When I was in his shoes, we idolized legendary Guardians like Captain Steel, but we were deathly afraid of the ones on the street. We called them "cans" and stayed as far away from them as possible. Some things never change.

Parade duty is a lousy shift, and as both a new grunt and a rockhead, I'd normally be assigned to it. But perimeter patrol is an even worse post, and we already had a shift this morning. Which means that, miraculously, I'm free to enjoy the festivities.

Founder's Day is the biggest holiday we have in Canyon City. Most people only have to work a half day, and there's a parade followed by fireworks after sunset. I looked forward to it for weeks when I was a kid. Now I forgot it was even happening. Growing up does funny things.

I duck under the familiar arched entrance to a huge table-top mesa and tramp up three flights of sandstone stairs. The mesa is honeycombed with shops, selling everything from salvaged bioelectronics to greenhouse-grown cucumbers. The smell of curry and fried onions from a food vendor makes my mouth water. Shopkeepers call out to me as I pass, attracted by the fine weave of my blue scarf.

They're wasting their breath. I certainly couldn't afford a scarf like this on my own. Even though I'm making a lot more now than when I worked the mines as a deep diver, my wages still go straight to the IEC to pay my family's debt. Despite what my dad told me about the IEC's perpetual-debt-for-cheap-labor scheme, I still have fantasies that some day I'll be able to pay it all off and be free of the IEC entirely.

I know I'm farting into the wind. But you've got to dream, right?

The entrance to Wayfinders looks just like I remember, a rusty door embedded in a chipped stone archway. Memories flood in as I approach the pitted metal. This place was my refuge. My home during all the years I didn't have one.

How many times did I push through this door, dreaming of winning a qualifier? Of someday becoming a Guardian? Now here I am, returning victorious, like some hero from a fairy tale.

The junk shop is dim inside, dimmer than I remember. It's smaller, dustier, and more cramped. Musty with the smell of old plastics and rusting metal. Then my eyes adjust to the light, and I see a familiar fringe of grey hair bent over a workbench.

Fin. My mentor. My friend.

"I'll be right there," he calls out, not bothering to look up from his work.

He looks the way I remember, and yet not. The same bald head, same unkempt hair, same multi-lensed glasses perched on his nose. Superficially, he's exactly the same. But he seems diminished some-how. Like I'm looking at him through the wrong end of a telescope.

I run my eyes over the rest of the shop. Same dusty shelves. Same heaps of salvaged bioelectric parts mounded here and there. My eyes stop on a familiar chair and my breath catches in my throat. I run my hand over the rough, rusted metal. My fingers come away brown, but I hardly notice. This is the chair I sat in when I won the Guardian Tour-nament qualifier. My journey began here.

Fin breaks my reverie.

"All right, what can I do for you?" He blinks up at me, spectacles pushed back on his bald scalp.

"I think you've already done enough."

His forehead furrows, then his eyes widen. "Theo? Is that you?"

"In the flesh. I told you I'd come back."

He laughs. "You've grown! And look at that scarf!" He scrutinizes me at arms' length. "Did you really do it? You survived the tournament?"

"I did."

"You're a Guardian now?"

"I am."

Fin shakes his head, eyes full of wonder. "I never thought I'd see the day. A rockhead becoming a Guardian. Sit down, tell me all about it. I'll make us some tea."

We catch up for a while, both of us trying to adjust to the strange change in our relationship. I tell him about the training competition and Merrimac. The friends I made, the enemies who tried to stop me.

Frowning, he nods. "I told you that place was dangerous."

"You were right. A lot of kids never made it. One of my crew has been in the hospital for months, unresponsive. They don't know if he'll ever come back." I pause, unsure how to bring up the thing I need to ask him. Finally, I just blurt it out. "Do you know how to get in touch with the Outsiders?"

His eyelids flutter with shock, then his brows draw down in suspicion. "Why would I know how to do that?"

"Come on, Fin. You know everybody. You've got to know something. Some way to send a message."

He watches me silently, his mouth pressed into a hard, wary line. I guess I don't blame him. I'm a Guardian now, and I come around asking about the Outsiders? If I want him to trust me, I'm going to have to trust him.

I pause, unsure how to tell him. If I should tell him at all. But the secret has been eating me up for months. I have to tell someone. I take a deep breath and reassure myself it's ok. I can trust Fin.

"Fin, my dad's alive."

He cocks an eyebrow. "Is that so?"

Something in his reaction plucks at me. He doesn't seem shocked, or even particularly surprised. Realization hits me like a sandstorm.

"You knew?"

Looking chagrined, he ducks his head, staring at the floor. "I guess I'm not much of an actor, eh?"

Hot fury boils up and I surge to my feet, my chair clattering into the metal shelves behind me.

"You knew my dad was alive and you never told me?" I'm shaking with outrage, my hands balled into fists.

Fin shrinks back, holding his palms up before him. "I'm sorry. It wasn't my secret to tell."

"But … how …" I fumble for words, unsure what I'm even trying to say. What do you say when you find out your mentor has been deceiving you for years? That the one thing you thought you could rely upon was built on a lie?

"I got a note from him about a week after he disappeared. He asked me to keep an eye on you," he says softly. "I did the best I could."

"And the best you could do was let me believe he was dead?" I blink back tears of rage and disappointment.

"Theo…"

Wayfinders is suddenly too small around me. Confining. All my memories here have been twisted, polluted by Fin's deception. I don't fit in this place anymore. I can't breathe.

Without another word, I push my way out of the shop, out into the crowd and the hot, dusty street. The heavy door slams shut behind me.

4

———

I push through the crowds, blinded by tears, paying no attention to where my feet are taking me. I only know I have to get away. Away from Wayfinders. Away from Fin. Away from the deception.

I can't believe he lied to me all those years. He knew my dad was alive. He knew and he didn't tell me. I thought he was my friend. How could he do that?

Wayfinders was my refuge. The one place in Canyon City I felt safe. Now it's just a dusty old shop full of lies.

My dad lied to me. Fin lied to me. Rory and Castle lied to me in Merrimac. My whole life has been filled with lies. Everyone I thought I could trust. Who's next? Shadow? Knott? Can I trust anyone?

The Founder's Day crowd is oppressive. Too many people, too many colors, too much joy and laughter. I turn away, ducking into an alley between two spires, moving away from the throng.

"Twist!"

A skinny boy with close-cropped black hair hurries up behind me. His face is familiar, but longer and leaner than I remember.

"Stick?"

He smiles, exposing yellow teeth. "You still remember your old friends, Twist?"

"Of course, I do. You've gotten tall."

"You're one to talk. Look at you, a real Guardian! I can't believe that fancy scarf!"

I finger the soft material self-consciously. Maybe I shouldn't have worn the scarf down here in Canyon City. It's too conspicuous.

"Yeah, things have changed a bit since last time I saw you."

We walk together, catching up. Stick's grown a lot. He's taller and more confident. His eyes are harder and full of secrets. A far cry from the wide-eyed kid who used to follow me around Wayfinders.

Still, it's good to see a familiar face. Someone to distract me, turn my mind away from Wayfinders and Fin's betrayal.

I don't pay attention to where we're going as Stick steers me down quieter and quieter streets. The hollowed-out spires grow closer together, pockmarked with windows. Dirty faces peer out at us as we pass. Refuse and fallen rocks gather in the gutters. Insects swarm in the piss-scented air.

It isn't until a deep voice calls out that I look up. Cold fear slides down my spine as I understand where we are.

A pair of broad-shouldered thumpers block the alley ahead of us, brandishing thick lengths of rusty rebar. One of them has tattoos on the back of his hands and a scar running across the bridge of his nose. Hedeg. Jepet's muscle.

I take a step back and glance behind me. Two more thumpers. Spines. Sweat slicks the back of my neck.

Stupid, wandering into back alleys without my armor. Letting self pity get the better of me. I rest my hand on the hilt of my warpknife, hidden beneath the tail of my shirt. The greicagin in its hilt tingles reassuringly against my hand. At least I've got that going for me if things get ugly.

"Stay behind me, Stick. I'll handle this."

"It's ok, Twist. They just want to talk."

It takes a moment for his words to sink in. Then I stare at him. "You brought me here on purpose?"

"It's ok, Twist." He backs away, his hands up, placating me. "Stay calm and nobody has to get hurt."

My betrayal flares up again, white hot. First Fin and now Stick. I guess it's true what they say: You can never go home again.

Hedeg steps forward. "Jepet wants a word."

"About what?"

I stand tall and try to keep my voice calm and authoritative. As if I'm the one in charge, not them. That's one thing I've learned being a Guardian. Half of being in charge is acting like you're in charge. If you believe it, other people tend to believe it too.

Hedeg's forehead wrinkles, his dark eyes narrowing. He's used to people cowering in front of him, and my tone and posture confuse him. His eyes flick to his fellow thumpers, checking the numbers. It's still four to one. Satisfied that he has the upper hand, Hedeg raises his rebar suggestively.

"That's Jepet's business. My business is to make sure you arrive at the conference table. Are you going to come quietly, or do we have to drag you?"

"I'll come."

It's better to go willingly and try to maintain the illusion of control. Even with my augments, I don't know if I could beat four trained fighters. I'd rather not show up to the meeting with cracked ribs and a busted skull.

They press in around me as we walk. Two in front, two in back. They don't lay their hands on me though. At least I've got that going for me.

I wonder what Jepet wants. I didn't even know he was still operating. The last time I dealt with him, he gave me a virus-infected dataspike that almost got me kicked out of Merrimac. To save myself, I had to give Merrimac's director, Castle, all the dirt on Jepet. I assumed his bones would be decorating an iron cage hanging from the wall by now. Yet apparently he's still free.

I don't know what that means, but I doubt it means anything good.

Maybe he knows I gave him up to Castle. Maybe the thumpers are taking me someplace quiet to bury a knife in my back. But if they wanted to do that, they could have done it back there in the alley. Unless Jepet wants to watch.

I chew the inside of my cheek as they lead me down a set of stone steps. A cheap yellow bulb illuminates an earthen cellar. Ancient, corroded support beams cross the ceiling, dropping flakes of rust onto a red dirt floor. The cool scent of rock is a welcome change from the reek of the alleys.

It's not the same cellar I came to the last time I paid Jepet a visit, but it looks like it's part of the same complex of tunnels. I wonder how extensive the tunnels really are. Last time I was here, Shadow told me they burrow beneath most of the west side of Canyon City. Could they be even more extensive than that? Could they stretch beyond the walls themselves?

Maybe I do want to talk to Jepet after all.

He looks just like I remember, perched on a pile of cushions behind a table covered with food, his bald head gleaming in the yellow light. He glances up from his feast as we enter, and his eyes go hard beneath his single spreading eyebrow. My throat tightens, anxiety rising up. I fight to keep my expression calm.

"Twist. How nice of you to join me."

"I wasn't given much of a choice."

He eyes me up and down, his lip curling with disdain. "So, you are a Guardian now. It seems our deal was beneficial to you. You owe me."

Searing anger burns away my fear. "I owe you? The virus you hid inside that dataspike almost got me expelled. I don't owe you anything."

"One favor, that was the deal."

"The deal didn't include me smuggling in a virus!"

He eyes me coldly. "Did it not? Perhaps you should read your contracts more carefully. There was nothing in our deal forbidding such a thing. It was merely a sweetener, in case you did not manage to become a Guardian after all. In that instance, I would have been out a sizable investment. I was merely hedging my bets. A wise business practice at all times."

"There was no contract, and you know it."

"Was there not? Then how do you know what was in the agreement?"

"Because I was in the room when we discussed it!"

"As was I." He takes a sip of tea, eyeing me over the rim. Then he smiles like a midfalcon about to swoop down upon its prey. "Memory is a fickle thing, I find. The memories of two people seldom agree. I will give you a business tip: Always get things in writing."

I grind my teeth, pressing my fingernails into my fists. I decide to change tactics.

"What do you know about the slave tunnels?"

His eyebrow raises, creating a long crease across his forehead.

"Slave tunnels? I know of no such thing."

His words say one thing, but their tone tells me another. He knows.

"I'm looking for someone. Can you put me in touch with the slavers?"

He laughs, a short bark of astonishment. "Put you in touch with the slavers? You still owe me a favor, and you have the audacity to ask for another?"

"I don't owe you anything. Your virus voids our previous deal."

I let my fingers stray toward the hilt of my warpknife, lifting the hem of my shirt so Jepet can see the weapon. His eyes turn hard, and his mouth flattens into a grim line. I talk fast, not giving him time to sic his thumpers on me.

"But I am willing to negotiate a new deal. What do you want in exchange for a meeting with the slavers?"

He stares at me, his expression frozen. I hold his gaze, doing my best to project confidence despite the tightness in my throat. My fingertips rest against the hilt of my warpknife. I can feel his thumpers leaning toward me. The moment stretches, balanced on the edge of a blade.

He takes another sip of his tea, his eyes never leaving mine.

"You will deliver first," he says finally. "I do not trust you otherwise."

I relax a tiny fraction. Maybe I'm not going to die today after all.

"Deliver what?"

"Information, what else? Information only a Guardian can learn."

I nod cautiously. "I'm listening."

"I have heard whispers that the Guardians are planning a crack-down on my people. I want details. Where, when, how many Guardians, everything. Bring me that and I will arrange the thing you ask."

I think about his offer. I doubt I can get the information myself, but I'm sure Shadow could. I hate to involve her, but she is the one who introduced me to Jepet in the first place.

It's asking a lot, though. I still owe her for the last time she helped me out.

But I also know she'll help if I ask her. And this is the best lead I've got to find Ianna.

I take a deep breath. "It's a deal."

"Excellent." He gives a satisfied predator's smile. "Hedeg will see you out."

"What about our contract? Didn't you just tell me to get everything in writing?"

His smile gets wider.

"Now where would be the fun in that?"

5

The parade is in full swing by the time I thread my way out of the back alleys. The early arrivers have been joined by the rest of the city, thousands of people thronging the streets. The noise is incredible: bands playing, children laughing, adults shouting and cheering, the rumble of heavy vehicles, and the explosions of fireworks overhead. For once Canyon City is alive, everyone smiling and happy, cheering the Guardians in their silver armor.

Seeing them up there, glinting bravely in the sun, I suddenly feel sad I've been left out. Earlier I was glad to have the rest of the day off. Now I feel like I'm missing something important. I should be up there. Getting cheered by the children.

Being given the afternoon off doesn't seem like a reward anymore, but a deliberate slight. Another way of telling me that even though I graduated from Merrimac, I'll always be a rockhead in the eyes of my fellow Guardians.

Well, dust them.

I'm secretly working against them anyway, biding my time until I get the signal from my dad and the Outsiders that it's time to turn against them. I'm a hidden flaw in their shining armor. I don't need their approval.

Still, watching them wave and smile, I think how nice it would be to be accepted. To have someone acknowledge I earned my place here, admit that I'm every bit as good as the Guardians who come from Sunrise.

I snort. Fat chance.

I push my way through the crowd, searching for Shadow. She said she'd be standing near Southspire, but finding her will be a challenge in this throng.

A couple of kids stick-fighting bounce off me, their faces flushed, eyes sparkling. I smile. I was that kid once, dreaming of being Captain Steel.

I guess in a way I am Captain Steel now.

Being a Guardian doesn't feel anything like I imagined it would, though. Maybe that's just life. By the time your dreams come true, they don't fit anymore. They're the dreams of someone younger.

One of the stick-fighting kids bumps into a gigantic armored Guardian. The Guardian grabs him by the arm and hauls him up into the air, yelling in his face and shaking him. The kid starts to cry, but the Guardian doesn't put him down, he just shakes him harder.

I set my jaw and push through the crowd toward them

"It's Guardians like you who give all of us a bad name." I grab his shoulder from behind, spinning him around. He's huge, almost half a meter taller than me, and twice as wide. Then I see his face, and my stomach squirms.

Ghengis drops the kid, who scrambles away into the crowd. He sneers down at me.

"Twist. Why am I not surprised? I'm sorry, was that your cousin? You dirty rockheads all look the same to me."

I haven't seen Ghengis since our final exam in Merrimac. He caught me in the middle of a sandstorm and picked me up as easily as he did that poor kid. Ghengis held me upside down by my ankle and slammed me into the ground over and over. I was helpless. I'd be dead right now if Knott hadn't showed up.

I swallow and lift my chin, trying not to let the fear show on my face.

"It's people like you who give the Guardians a bad name. It's Founders Day, and you're terrorizing children like some street thug."

"No, it's you that gives us a bad name." Ghengis pokes a massive finger into my chest, knocking me back a step. "My father was a Guardian, and my grandfather. I know what it means to wear this armor. You are a nothing but a dusty street rat. You know nothing."

I want to punch him in his smug mouth. I want to draw my warpknife and ram it down his throat.

Ghengis sees the urge in my face and smiles. He spreads his arms wide.

"Go ahead, Twist. Take a swing. I'll give you the first shot."

"Twist." Jmini's voice is urgent in my ear. "This isn't the time or place. And I'd like to point out that the brute is wearing armor, while you are not. Walk away."

He's right, of course. Ghengis would destroy me on a good day. Right now, when I'm not even armored? I haven't got a fly's chance in a storm.

Still I stand there with my eyes locked onto his, shaking with rage. Knowing something and being able to do it are not the same thing.

Fortunately, a new voice breaks our standoff.

"Well, if it isn't everyone's favorite rockhead."

Rory steps up next to Ghengis, bringing a new rush of emotions and memories. My eyes go to the shining metal hand that grips the barrel of his cannon. Rory was part of my crew, until he betrayed us. I gave him that metal hand when I severed his real hand at the wrist with my warpknife.

I bring my eyes back to his, but he saw my glance. His lips flatten into a thin, angry line.

"That's right, stare at the freak hand." He holds it up and waggles his fingers. The metal flashes in the sun. "You owe me for this, Twisty. I'll be coming to collect when you least expect it."

"When I least expect it? Like the way you betrayed our team during the final exam?" I shake my head in disgust, looking from him to Ghengis. "You two deserve each other."

I keep my head high as I turn and walk away. The back of my neck itches, and every second I expect to feel Rory's cannon blast between my shoulder blades. I don't think he'd actually shoot me, not here, not with all these people around. But the feeling persists all the same.

My emotions churn as I'm finally swallowed up by the crowd. Rory bothers me more than Ghengis. I mean, Ghengis is a psychopath, but he was always that way. I expect it from him.

Rory was part of my crew. I thought he was my friend. His betrayal is a bruise deep inside my chest.

I make my way across the wide plaza around Southspire. After the Mesa, Southspire is the tallest spire in Canyon City. A lot of Canyon City's bigwigs live in the apartments up there, looking down on the rest of us.

The parade pauses here, and I see the governor making his way up onto a platform to give a speech. He's got a sweeping silver mustache, and hair so perfect it looks sculpted. His silver and red ceremonial uniform is spotless, and his crisp, polished buttons gleam in the sun. He moves with confidence, like a man used to others giving way before him.

It's not the governor who catches my eye, though. A handful of assistants huddle at the far edge of the platform, looking self-important and uncomfortable at being surrounded by so many commoners. One of them is tall, with ash-blond hair and wide shoulders. A cold look is stamped on his perfect features.

Octav.

I feel the blood drain from my face.

That's impossible. He's dead. I killed him during our final exam at Merrimac.

Yet there he is, standing at the edge of the platform. One of the governor's aids. Looking as arrogant and smug as ever.

"It's not Octav." Shadow materializes out of the crowd beside me.

"It's not?"

"No, it's his brother Julius. The one who didn't make it into Merrimac, remember? He was eliminated in one of the qualifiers."

I swallow. Oh, I remember all right. I remember because I was the one who eliminated him.

"He's the governor's assistant?"

"After he didn't make it into the academy, he went into politics instead. Word is, he's a real rising star. I hear they're grooming him to be the next governor."

Julius the next governor? That would not be good news for the person who knocked him out of the qualifying tournament. And killed his brother. I wonder if he remembers me?

Just then, his pale blue eyes latch onto me in the crowd. They narrow and his mouth twists into an ugly scowl. I swallow with difficulty, my mouth gone dry.

He remembers all right.

Fortunately, the governor chooses that moment to step up to the microphone, preventing Julius from vaulting off the platform and cutting me down then and there.

The governor smiles, waving at the crowd. He opens his mouth to speak … and the podium explodes.

The force of the blast lifts me off my feet and hurls me to the ground, along with most of the crowd. A high-pitched whine in my ears mutes the screams that fill the air. I struggle to pull my limbs free of the tangled bodies in the dust. Acrid smoke fills my nose, burning my lungs.

I pull my scarf up over my face as my stunned mind turns, trying to make sense of what happened.

The podium exploded.

There was a bomb.

I struggle through the smoke in what I hope is the direction of the podium. The ground around me is strewn with bodies. People screaming in fear and pain. They're starting to panic, pushing one another aside in their haste to get away. I see a little girl lying senseless, blood covering her face. People are stumbling over her, stepping on her.

I stop and protect her with my body. Gather her in my arms and cast about for a safe place to set her down.

Shadow tugs at my sleeve. Her voice is distant, little more than a whisper beneath the high tone in my ears.

"This way."

She leads me around to the west side of the Southspire. This area was shielded from the blast, and there's a clear space on the ground. I lay the girl against the base of the spire and check her injuries. She's got a long gash across her scalp, right above her forehead. Blood falls in sheets down her face. I tear a strip of cloth from my scarf and use it as a makeshift bandage. So much for my new scarf. The girl needs it more than I do right now.

I turn and find Shadow dragging a woman over by the armpits. I help her get the woman settled, then fight my way back out into the panicked crowd. Everywhere I turn, bloody people are crying out in pain and fear. I forget all about the governor. Other people need my help.

Shadow and I repeat our operation over and over, carrying wounded people to our makeshift triage at the base of Southspire. By the time I pause to catch my breath, we've gathered dozens. I slump against Southspire, my exhausted limbs heavy as the stone against my back. Even augmented strength has its limits. My clothes and hands are covered with blood. My fine scarf has been reduced to tatters.

And still more people cry out for help.

6

Castle rips us all a new one.

"The governor was killed on your watch! You're a disgrace to the Guardians." He glares around the room, making us squirm in our chairs. I feel like I'm back in Merrimac. A know-nothing student all over again.

We're sitting in a briefing room on the seventh floor of the Mesa. It's a shallow bowl carved from red sandstone, with thin striations of white and black swirling within the walls. Even the chairs have been carved from the stone, neat rows rising organically from the floor as part of the bowl itself. Despite this, my chair is surprisingly comfortable, the cool rock shaped and smooth beneath my legs.

Which isn't to say that I'm comfortable right now. At all.

It doesn't seem fair that Castle got promoted after our graduation ceremony. I was looking forward to leaving him back in Merrimac. Instead he's the new Commandant. The Commander of every Guardian in Canyon City. Barking away at us the same as always.

He pins me with an icy stare.

"And I don't want to hear about how it wasn't your fault because you were off-duty. A Guardian is always on duty. Every single one of you shoulders the blame for this."

He glares around the room again, making sure everybody feels the weight of his wrath.

"The Outsiders have gone too far this time. They've embarrassed the entire colony. Plans are being drawn up as we speak. We will no longer suffer the existence of these vermin. We're going to exterminate them like the pests they are."

"Yeah! Burn 'em all!" A couple of rows over, Rory cheers like he's at a dueling pit, pumping his fist in the air.

A complicated storm of emotions goes through me every time I see his metal hand: sadness, regret, anger, and satisfaction. I don't feel great about maiming him, but I don't regret it either. He got what was coming to him.

It looks like he's landed on his feet just fine, anyway. He's part of Ghengis's squad now, which is probably where he should have been to begin with. If anyone deserves each other, it's those two.

Rory catches me staring at him and extends his metal hand as if he's showing it off for my benefit. Then he turns the back of the hand toward me and curls all the fingers down but one. Cute.

On the way to our barracks, we're a silent, sullen bunch. I imagine most of my fellow Guardians are thinking about the dressing down we just suffered. Or maybe they're thinking about the death of the Governor and are looking forward to revenge.

I'm silent for a different reason. One of those Outsiders is my dad. I'm a mole within the Guardians. Waiting for my chance to make a difference in the fight against the IEC. Waiting to get revenge on the evil bastards who killed my mother and sent my sister some place I still haven't been able to find.

I'm supposed to keep my head down and not do anything suspicious. Wait until they decide to activate me.

But if this offensive is successful, that time may never come. The Outsiders need to know what's heading their way. I have to warn them.

But how? They didn't tell me how to get in touch with them. They only told me to wait for instructions. Fin is the only person I can think of who might have contacts outside the wall. But there's no way I'm going back to that liar.

I grind my teeth as I walk, racking my brain. Waiting is not good enough. There's got to be some way to contact them.

But first, I have to have something to tell them. Which means I've got to see the plans being drawn up for the offensive.

As luck would have it, I need to break into the central system to fulfill my deal with Jepet. As long as I'm stealing information about one raid, it shouldn't be hard to steal information about two.

I hope.

If I get caught, I'll be charged with espionage and expelled from the Guardians. I'll probably end up in a cage on the wall.

I can't think about that. I knew the risks when I made the deals. All that matters is how I'm going to do it.

I sidle up next to Shadow as we walk down the hall. I keep my voice low.

"We need to talk. Alone."

She raises an eyebrow and steers me to a quiet alcove.

I glance around, making sure we won't be overheard. "I made another deal with Jepet."

Shadow shakes her head.

"You never learn, do you? How'd the last deal work out for you?"

"I'd like to point out it was you who facilitated that deal."

"Sure, and it was a mistake. I acknowledge that. But at least I know better than to throw good credits after bad."

"It's important, Shadow. It's about my sister."

She scowls and folds her arms over her chest. "It's always important. You know you're risking your life here? My life? You've been looking for months, Twist, and you've found nothing. Maybe she's gone. Maybe she's dead. Have you considered that?"

I set my jaw and curl my fingers into fists. "She's not dead. I won't believe that until I've personally turned over every single rock in Canyon City."

We stare at each other for a minute, then she sighs and looks away.

"Fine, I'll help you. Remind me again why we're friends?"

"Because no one else will have us. We're a couple of rockheads sinking in a sea of Sunrisers."

"So you're saying we're castaways?" She laughs. "It all makes sense now. Castaways don't have a wide selection of friends to choose from."

"Nope. It's me or the flesh-eating cannibals."

"Sometimes you make the cannibals look pretty appealing, Twist. OK, what do you need?"

She listens closely as I tell her what I have to do. I don't tell her about stealing the attack plan for the Outsiders. That's my own private risk.

She nods when I'm done.

"All right. Give me a day or two to scope it out. I'll get back to you."

Warm relief floods through me, and for a second I want to tell her everything. About my dad, the Outsiders, the whole strike. It's a lot to carry on my own, and I want to share it with her so much I can taste it. But I swallow it down. Telling her would only endanger her.

I smile and pat her on the shoulder instead. "Thanks, Shadow. You're the best friend I've got. You know that, right?"

She scoffs and pushes me away. "I'm the only friend you've got, Twist. Being the best in a field of one isn't a very high bar to clear."

Still, she smiles, and I can tell the words mean something to her. I'm glad. She deserves a lot more than that. But words are all I have to give right now.

7

———————

I'm sitting in the cafeteria chewing my lip, looking out at the night through the huge windows that cover the entire wall. Neither moon has risen yet, and a thick blanket of stars twinkle above. It's nearly winter, and the cold shifts the starlight sapphire blue. The lights of Canyon City glow a warm counterpoint below.

I don't sit near the glass. I've gotten used to being up seven stories, but that doesn't mean I like it. Heights still make my knees weak. I'll admire the view from a safe distance, thank you very much.

I sip steaming matte through a metal straw, brooding. I'd never had the bitter drink before I became a Guardian. Now it's one of my favorite things. It's even worth braving the view from the cafeteria for.

"Ugh. I don't know how you can drink that stuff." Kass slips into the chair opposite me. The cinnamon scent of her shampoo drifts across the table. She looks the same as she did in Merrimac: same dark curls, same red-gold skin, same piercing blue eyes, same perfect lips and smile.

In other words, completely stunning.

I still don't know why she spends her time with a rockhead like me. One of these days she's going to come to her senses and dump me. Until then I'm doing my best to enjoy the ride while it lasts.

I grin at her. "It's pretty good once you get used to it. You have to give it a chance."

She shudders. "Not happening. I'll stick to coffee, thank you very much."

"It's your loss."

"No, it's your loss. Your poor taste buds are dying one by one."

I just smile and breathe her in. I don't get to see her as much as I'd like, but she still comes down to see me a couple of times a week. Amazing.

I say "comes down" because she's been assigned to the command section upstairs. Got her junior lieutenant bar and everything. So hanging out with me is slumming in more ways than one.

Shadow says I should be up in command too. Our team won the Guardian Tournament, after all. But I know that's pushing things a bit too far. It's a miracle they let us rockheads into the Guardians at all. There's no way they'd ever put one of us in command.

Which is fine with me. Being in charge of a bunch of Sunrisers who resent my every command does not sound like my idea of a good time. I'm fine being a grunt.

Better than fine, in fact. Compared to my former life mining greicagins in Papa Grady's crew, being stationed up here in the Mesa is jelly-easy. I've got my own room in the barracks and everything. It's barely big enough for a bed and a small closet for my uniforms, but it's got four strong walls and a door, and it's all mine. As far as I'm concerned, that's one step from paradise.

I know my happiness comes with a price. The good life up here rests on the backs of every rockhead working their fingers to the bone down there in the dust.

My dad's got it even worse, hiding in caves out in the scablands with the Outsiders. Hunted and living in fear.

And Ianna… I don't even want to think about all the horrible things that could have happened to my little sister in the years since they separated us. The possibilities were grim enough before I found out about the slavers. I shudder to think what might have happened to her now.

"Why the long face?" Kass strokes my cheekbone with her fingertips. My skin grows warm at the contact.

"Oh, no reason. Just thinking."

"Maybe this will cheer you up."

She pushes a flat white box across the table. Red ribbon loops around the sides and gathers in a neat bow on top.

"You got me a present?"

"Obviously. Open it, rockhead."

My fingers shake as I try to untie the delicate ribbon without tearing it. Kass snorts impatiently.

"Just tear it off. It's only ribbon."

But I continue my slow, careful unpicking. It may be only ribbon to her, but to me the perfect ribbon is as precious as whatever lies inside the box.

I finally get the ribbon untied and lift the lid with reverent hands. Inside the box is a beautiful new scarf. It's blue, like my last one, but the weave is much, much finer. It's so nice I'm afraid to touch it.

"This is for me?" My eyes are as big as dinner plates.

"No, it's for your crew. Yes, it's for you, rockhead. Pick it up." She's smiling, pleased by my reaction.

I hesitantly pinch the fabric and rub it between my fingers. The cloth is soft as down.

"This is too nice. I can't wear this."

"You can, and you will. You destroyed your last scarf helping people. You deserve a new scarf."

"But…"

"No buts." She steps around the table, takes the scarf from the box, and wraps it around my neck. I stand perfectly still as the smooth fabric settles against my skin. I've never even been near a scarf this nice before.

Kass laughs at my expression. "It's not going to bite you, Twist."

"It's so delicate. I'm afraid if I breathe on it too hard it'll fall apart."

"Just because it's soft doesn't mean it's delicate. That scarf is tougher than your last one was. I expect you to wear it. That's an order."

"Yes ma'am, Lieutenant sir." I snap off a mock salute.

"That's better. Now, are you ready to go have some fun?"

"Fun?"

"There are duels in honor of the governor's memory in the Quarry tonight. Instructor Asa is participating. It's going to be warp-sharp. Come on, you look like you could use some fun."

"But…"

"I said, 'no buts.' I'm getting you out of this dump."

She grabs my hand, pulls me from my chair, and drags me out into the night.

8

The Quarry is packed by the time we arrive, the light of the just risen moon, Hera, pink over the crowd. The night air is crisp and cold, making my breath steam from my lips. It's getting colder by the day, right on the cusp of winter. I wrap my new scarf tight, grateful for the insulation.

The Quarry is an old surface mine that was closed down decades ago. Now the tiered walls have been smoothed and leveled, making a perfect seating area for watching duels.

Duels are the preferred sport of Canyon City's elite. Warpknife duelists are celebrities, and the big names draw crowds. There must be a big name on the card tonight, because the quarry is full all the way to the upper tiers.

"Who's dueling?" I let Kass pull me toward the lower tiers. Her fingers are strong and callused in mine. Warrior's fingers.

"There are nine bouts, as tradition dictates. The undercard is nothing special, but Asa is in the eighth duel. The governor was her uncle. The final bout is Mince Maul versus Winter Went."

I whistle softly. Mince Maul and Winter Went are two of the top-ranked duelists in the Five Canyons. The dead governor must have been one of their sponsors.

There are nine levels to the quarry, mirroring the nine bouts. Ten if you count the mesa at the top. Kass leads me out onto the second tier from the bottom, the one reserved for administrators and Guardians. It feels weird looking up at all the rockheads filling the tiers above me. Even though I've been a Guardian for months now, I still feel like an imposter, pretending to be someone I'm not. I can't shake the nagging feeling that any minute one of the ushers is going to realize I don't belong on the second tier and ask me to leave.

They won't, of course. The chip embedded beneath the skin of my wrist clearly states that I am a Guardian, entitled to all privileges. I just wish someone would rewrite my brain, so I'd believe it too.

The tier below us holds the cream of society. Off to our left, the highest officials of the government are seated inside a box draped with black bunting. I suck in a breath when I see Julius sitting there. Maybe they really are grooming him to be governor. Perhaps me eliminating him from the qualifier was a blessing in disguise.

I doubt he'd see it that way, though. And I did still kill his twin brother during our final exam. He won't be thanking me anytime soon.

"How did Julius end up in that box anyway?"

Kass rolls her eyes.

"Family connections."

"So he didn't have enough connections to get into the Guardian Tournament, but he had enough to become the governor's protege? How does that work?"

"It's complicated. Saying he didn't have the connections to get into Merrimac is wrong. He could have gotten in through his family connections, but he chose not to use them. He figured he'd have no problem winning the qualifier, and then he could still use his family favors to fast track his career after graduation. You derailed that plan when you beat him in the qualifier. At that point, it was too late to use his connections to get in. He'd taken his gamble and lost. So he used them to become one of the governor's aids instead. The governor took a liking to him, and here we are."

"I guess fortune favors the rich and powerful."

"Every time."

The quarry hushes as the first set of duelists step into the circle and salute the crowd with their warpknives. The first few bouts are mostly trainees and old heads. Wanna-bes and has-beens. The winner is the first to three touches, but the undercard fighters keep their warpknives in safe mode, so the touches are little more than shallow scratches.

The crowd grows restless as the competitors shuffle in and out of the tunnel to the dressing room without major injury. They came to see blood.

Finally, the duelists for the sixth bout emerge, wrapped in sleek armor. The crowd perks up and cheers echo across the Quarry. The real fighting is about to begin.

I see a bulky, furtive figure slip into the tunnel behind the exiting fighters. I recognize Jepet's bald scalp even all the way across the Quarry. What's he doing here? Suspicion tickles my brain.

"I'll be right back."

Kass nods vaguely, intent on the duelists entering the circle.

I make my way around to the tunnel. The guard at the entrance scans my chip and waves me through.

Inside the hollowed stone tunnel, the noise of the crowd becomes something else. Individual voices are swallowed, transformed into a collective growl. The earth shakes with the thunder of thousands of feet stomping in unison. It's like being inside the belly of a giant, or a mine during an earthquake. It makes me feel very small.

I follow the reek of old sweat and blood down the tunnel. I pass closed doors with names on them: Mink Maul, Winter Went, and others. The individual dressing rooms of the stars. At the end of the hall, I find the fighters from the earlier bouts in a large, communal dressing room. They sit slumped on benches, looking tired and defeated, while ragged boys unwrap the tape from their wrists and ankles. From the beaten expressions on their faces, it's impossible to separate the winners of the bouts from the losers.

I stop in the shadows just outside the doorway, scanning the room for Jepet. He's off to one side, talking with a heavily scarred man whose crooked nose looks like it's been broken too many times to count. The man looks familiar and I stare at his profile, trying to recall where I've seen him before.

Finally, it hits me. The man is Gorky Fall, a well-known trainer of duelists. The low-ranked fighters must be part of his stable.

Why do they all look so defeated then? And what business does he have with Jepet? I need to hear what they're saying. Fortunately, even though I'm not wearing my armor, I'm still a Guardian. I've got resources.

I slip in my earcones.

"Jmini, amplify that conversation for me."

"Aye aye, Capitan."

Jepet's voice comes through my earcones, as clear as if he were standing next to me. I see him slip a wad of folded credits over to Gorky.

"Here's your cut. Well done, your fighters did as they were told. A profitable night for everyone."

It takes me a minute to figure out what he means. Then disgust twists my stomach. The duels were fixed, the winners of the low-ranked bouts predetermined. Jepet placed bets on the winners, and both he and Gorky made money from the wagers. No wonder the fighters look defeated. They weren't really fighting at all.

"When will you deliver the new kids? I'm still waiting for the boys and girls I ordered." Gorky runs a thick thumb across his chin, his eyes intent.

Jepet waggles his hand dismissively.

"You'll have them by the end of the week."

I'm confused. Doesn't Gorky get assigned apprentices through the IEC, the same way Papa Grady used to? Why would Jepet be bringing him children?

My stomach drops as realization hits me. Maybe he's not being assigned new apprentices at all. Maybe he's buying new slaves.

My anger flares. Jepet has been playing me. Of course he can put me in touch with the slavers. He is one of the slavers.

I step into room. "Jepet! Funny meeting you here."

Everyone freezes, dozens of pairs of eyes locking onto me. Jepet scowls, his massive brow lowering over his eyes.

"You shouldn't be here, Twist."

"I could say the same of you. I'm pretty sure the sign on the door says 'Staff Only'. You don't look like staff to me."

"Gorky is an old friend. I came down to say hello."

"Friend? I wish I had friends like you. Seems like you give your friends a lot of money."

Jepet spreads his hands wide. "I owed him some money for a favor, that's all. Now we're all squared away."

"Squared away except for the new kids you're going to be delivering. You've been playing me, Jepet. Telling me you'd arrange a meeting with the slavers, when you're the guy I've been wanting to talk to all along, aren't you?"

"This is not the time or place to discuss our business. Come see me at my office."

"No, we'll discuss this now."

My warpknife blazes, a green crescent in my hand. The power of the shard in the hilt runs through my arm, tingling all the way up into my shoulder. It makes me feel strong. Invincible.

Jepet sighs. "Drawing that in here was a mistake, kid. Gorky, take care of this problem, would you?"

Too late, I realize what I've done. I assumed Jepet wouldn't dare assault a Guardian in a public place. But this place isn't really public. Everyone in the room is owned by Gorky. And Gorky is owned by Jepet.

My implants shoot adrenaline into my heart, and Jmini activates the tracking system in my eyes, labeling every threat in the room with red tags. The world slows down, coming into sharp focus. In addition to Gorky and Jepet, I count twelve trained duelists, and almost as many trainers and towel boys. The duelists have their hands on their warpknives and their eyes on Gorky, waiting for the word.

"Maybe we'd better continue this discussion another time."

I edge back towards the door. I'm closer to the exit than most of them. There's only a trainer, a pair of towel boys, and a bearded duelist between me and the tunnel.

Gorky barks, "Stop him."

The trainer lunges toward me, and I spin with inhuman speed, swinging my warpknife in an arc. He cries out, tumbling aside. I let loose a banshee yell and charge the towel boys. They dive out of my way, tripping over themselves in their haste to avoid the edge of my knife.

That leaves only the bearded duelist. I don't recognize him, but the scars on his cheeks and neck tell me he's been at this a long time. He blocks the door, balancing on the balls of his feet, warpknife ready.

I check my peripheral display. Five more duelists are closing in behind me. Not good. I've got to get past this guy, before I'm overwhelmed by their numbers.

I feint high and thrust low, but he's ready for it, parrying my attack easily. I follow that up with a diagonal slash, but he steps out of range and I slash air.

The other duelists are coming in fast. Jmini's display says they'll be on me in less than two seconds. I have to get out of here now.

I put everything I have into a furious attack, slashing, thrusting and feinting in a dizzying series of moves. The old fighter's good: He manages to parry the first three. But he can't keep up with the speed of my implants, and I catch him in the face with a hilt punch. Blood explodes from his nose. I shoulder him aside and lunge for the door.

A hand clamps around my left bicep.

As I turn to slash at it, someone kicks me right below the ribs. I cry out and stagger, raising my guard toward this new threat. But before I can even focus on them, someone else clips me on the temple. The floor rushes up and cold stone slams into my face.

I try to push myself up, but the boots are coming down now, pounding into my ribs, my shoulders, my legs. The beating has begun, and there's nothing I can do except take it.

Eventually, they exhaust their fury. I'm vaguely aware of being carried out through a back tunnel. I have a brief sensation of flying, then the ground slams into me again. Dust and blood fill my mouth. I think I'm just going to lie here for a while.

9

I t takes a while, but I eventually find my feet and stumble away. My new scarf has blood on it. Everything hurts.

All of Canyon City must be crammed into the Quarry; two blocks away the streets are empty and quiet. Which suits me fine. I need to think, and a screaming crowd is the last place I want to be right now.

"Jmini, send Kass a message. Say I felt sick or something. I had to go."

"Very smooth." Jmini's voice is heavy with disapproval. "I'm sure she'll believe that."

"If you can think of a better excuse, send that. I can't think about it right now. I'll apologize to her later."

My thoughts churn. Jepet is a slaver. He might know where Ianna is. But how do I get that information from him? I can't shake him down; I've seen how well that works out. And I'm not sure how my performance back there in the dressing room will affect our deal. At this point, I wouldn't be surprised if he puts a contract out on my head.

Jepet is not someone you want as an enemy. My rash decision to confront him has made finding my sister a whole lot more difficult. Not to mention more dangerous.

Spines.

Maybe I can use Gorky against him somehow? My head is spinning with too many possibilities. I need time to work them all out.

The iron cages hanging from the city wall creak overhead as I pass. The miserable convicts within them are probably the only people in Canyon City who feel worse than I do right now. Their groans and sobs blend with the eerie moaning of the wind. One poor mad soul laughs hysterically.

I climb the stairs to the top of the wall and lean on the parapet, looking out over the moonlit canyon beyond. The cold breeze soothes my aching head. The sandy canyon floor stretches pink in Hera's light, the walls ghostly and shadowed. The second moon, Eros, is a rising blue glow on the horizon. Spires thrust up here and there, wind-carved and twisted, like gnarled fangs waiting to pierce any who venture too close.

Who first looked at this place and thought it would be a good home for humans? The scablands aren't a place for nourishing life. They're a proving ground for nasty things. Reaper plants and Horrors. Spines and thorns and claws and teeth.

My dad is out there somewhere, maybe my sister too. To protect them, will I have to become a horror myself? Have I already?

A horrible screech pierces the night and I stagger, clutching at my ears. Floodlights pop on below, illuminating a massive Rock Horror outside the gate. Metallic green highlights flash along the length of its black carapace as it flexes two meter-long crystalline pincers. Their serrated edges are razor sharp and deadly. Rage and despair rise off it like smoke.

A dozen silver-armored Guardians come boiling out of the gate, warpknives drawn and glowing. The big cannons mounted on top of the wall stay silent, useless against the creature's carapace.

The Horror is huge, fast, desperate, and deadly. The Guardians are professional killers who have the advantage of numbers and high-tech weaponry.

It's no contest. The Horror shrieks and lunges, slashing through armor like cloth, leaving men writhing in pools of blood. But the

Guardians are too numerous. Working together, they cut the Horror down with brutal efficiency.

I find myself clinging to the parapet, my legs weak. Tears stream down my face. I felt it. Just like in the mine. The Horror's pain and fear. The hate and despair. As if I was being cut to pieces along with it.

A soft cackle comes out of the darkness.

"You feel it too—don't you, tin man? You know they're not just animals."

I turn and find a ragged figure sitting in the shadows. In Hera's dim light I can only make out vague features: a strong hook of a nose, deep-set eyes, hair as tangled and wild as lanbrush.

I step back, tensing.

"Who are you? What are you doing up here?"

The cackle sounds again. "I go where I like."

"You didn't answer my question. Who are you?"

"Who I am is unimportant. What is important is the Horrors. Why do you think they keep attacking when they know it's certain death?"

The figure relaxes on the edge of the parapet, as if we were sitting in a kitchen having tea. I keep my fingers near the hilt of my warp-knife. The old crackpot isn't going to catch me off guard.

"They don't know it's certain death. They're brainless killing machines."

"Are they? Then why the sorrow? Why the despair?"

"I don't know what you're talking about."

The figure smiles, his mouth a dark crescent in the night. "I think you do."

I eye the old beggar warily. I've never told anyone I feel the emotions of the Horrors. They'd think I was crazy.

"So what if I do? It doesn't change anything."

"But it could. The weight of conviction can move mountains."

"Do you always talk in riddles? Or do I get special treatment?"

"Simply ask yourself why. Why throw themselves against the wall again and again? Is it suicide? What kind of despair could lead to that?"

I scowl at him. "I've got more important things to worry about than a bunch of suicidal Horrors."

"Do you? What if the Horrors are the key to everything?"

He gestures out beyond the wall and my eyes follow, down to where the clean-up crew is hacking off chunks of meat for disposal, leaving dark stains on the sand. The breeze carries the putrid scent of death.

Despite myself, my curiosity is piqued.

What if the stranger is right? What if the Horrors are a bigger part of the puzzle? I think back to the Rock Horror we killed in the abandoned mine. What was it doing down there? Why had it been attacking settlers and supply trains? Could it have had a reason beyond simple animal viciousness?

I shake my head. No. The whole thing is ridiculous. If Horrors were more than animals, the first scientific survey would have discovered that. They would have never allowed colonists on Greica in the first place.

I turn to say as much to the ragged stranger, but the parapet is empty. I whirl around, warpknife springing to my hand. All I find are shadows and wind.

10

I don't sleep well, haunted by dreams of Horrors and slaves and duelists with warpknives hacking me apart. In the morning, I'm woken by a summons to an emergency briefing. I grab a cup of matte and stumble down the hall, my mind fuzzy and full of half-remembered dreams. Kass catches me in the hall outside the meeting room.

"What happened to you last night? Jmini's message said you were sick?"

"Oh, uh, yeah. I must have eaten something that didn't agree with me." I yawn and knuckle sleep crust from my eyes.

Kass brushes her fingertips down my cheek, her forehead creased with concern. "Why is your face bruised? What's going on?"

"It's nothing. I, uh, fell down some stairs."

Her eyes flare. "If you're going to ditch me and lie to my face, you should at least try to be more convincing." She turns on her heel and stomps away.

"Kass…"

I don't really try to stop her. What would be the point? I don't want to get her involved in my trouble with Jepet.

Maybe I should tell her that? I scrub my hands over my face in an effort to jolt my tired mind into motion. Ugh. It's too early for decisions like this. Maybe later.

Shadow raises an eyebrow at me as I stumble into the briefing room and collapse into the seat next to her. Knott looms in the next chair over, silent and solid as a gargoyle.

"What happened to your face?"

"Don't ask."

Knott leans forward in her chair. "You need a bodyguard?"

I ignore her and bury my face in the cup, letting the steam caress my cheeks. I just want half an hour to sit here and sip my matte and wake up. Is that too much to ask?

"Take your seats."

Castle bursts into the room, bright eyed and vigorous, looking like he's just run ten kilometers. Knowing him, he probably has.

I stifle a groan and do my best to look attentive.

Castle grips the podium with both hands and spears us with his wintry blue eyes.

"We are taking the fight to the Outsiders. We have allowed these terrorists to exist for long enough. Today we are launching an offensive that will eradicate the Outsiders from the face of Greica once and for all. To that end, we're developing a new type of weapon we call the Tunnel Diver."

A projection appears in the air beside him. The thing is tapered and cone-shaped, like a giant mole. Except it also has giant rotating teeth at the front, ready to chew through any passageways too small to pass. It looks sleek and monstrous.

"The Tunnel Diver is the key to rooting out the Outsiders. With it, we can follow those vermin wherever they may hide. No longer will the area beneath the surface belong to the enemy."

At first glance, it seems like a good idea. The five canyons are riddled with natural caves, crevices, and thousands of abandoned mines. The underground has been the Outsider's biggest advantage in their struggle; take that away and they could be in big trouble.

"We'll be launching this offensive as soon as the Tunnel Divers are ready to go. I don't have an exact date, but it will be soon. So check your equipment and be ready to launch at a moment's notice." He bares his big, square teeth in a fierce smile. "Dismissed."

I rise from my chair, my mind shocked awake. This could change everything. The Outsiders need to be warned.

As everyone filters out of the room, I pull Shadow aside in the hallway. Knott lingers nearby. Far enough away to give us privacy, but close enough to stand guard.

"Have you figured out how to do that thing I asked?"

She shakes her head. "No, not yet. The central data system is heavily secured. I don't know if I'll be able to do it. You might have to make a different deal with Jepet."

I scowl. "Jepet's goons gave me these bruises. The only deal I'm making with him is the one where I kick down his door and trade him his life for information."

"Sounds good to me. Where and when?"

I was half-joking, but Shadow seems serious. Could we really kick in Jepet's door? The thought is tempting.

"We're talking about a man with a lot of bodyguards here." I say slowly.

"So what? They don't have Guardian armor, do they?"

"Or me." Knott's voice comes from right behind me. I start and look up to find her smirking.

Huh. Maybe we really could do this. It's certainly a more direct route to Ianna. A grin creeps toward my ears.

"You two are crazy, you know that?"

Shadow grins back. "Crazy like a fox."

"Do you know where Jepet's doing business these days?"

She rolls her eyes at me. I hold my palms up in surrender.

"Ok, it was a stupid question. When do we want to do this?"

"Well, we're not on shift until this evening. I'm not doing anything right now…" Shadow cocks an eyebrow at me.

Knott nods her agreement.

I hesitate. I'd love to suit up and bust in Jepet's door, but I have to get the Outsiders some intel on the assault. If they aren't warned, it could be a slaughter.

Spines. The data I want now isn't for Jepet, it's for my dad and the Outsiders. For the thousandth time I think about coming clean, telling Shadow everything. She's my best friend, she deserves to know the risks.

And for the thousandth time, I don't do it. If I get caught, she's the first person they'll question. If she knows anything at all, they'll take her down along with me. The only way to protect her is to keep her in the dark.

I have to find another way.

"Meet me by Southspire in three hours. I've got something I need to take care of first."

I gulp down the last of my matte and head for room 212.

11

Room 212 used to be part of the sick ward. Just a standard bed and a medrig for monitoring the patient's status. Over the last few months it has slowly evolved to fit the changing needs of the room's single patient. Now room 212 is a maze of machinery, a dim labyrinth of humming cables, blinking status lights, and whirring fans.

Grab lies at the heart of it all, wires and tubes sprouting from his body, as much a part of the maze as the rest of the machines. After he kamikazied his Hummingbird into Ghengis during our final exam, his body never recovered. He'll probably be stuck in this bed forever, machines pumping his blood in and out of his veins, inflating and deflating his lungs like bellows. He was already half-machine before the accident. Now it's more like ninety percent.

The maze reeks of old sweat and hot machinery. The scent of Grab, seeping into the walls with each passing day. I don't hold it against him. The nurses do their best with the sponge baths, but it's hard to maneuver around the dozens of tubes and wires tying Grab into his nest.

His empty eye sockets turn toward me as I pick my way through the maze to his bed. Wires run into his skull hooked directly to his optic nerves, letting him watch me through the cameras mounted in the corners of the room. Every day his body does less and less, and the machines do more and more.

His mind is another matter. His mind is not trapped in this room with his stinking body and dusty machines. His mind roams free over the datanets, like an imfalcon soaring on thermal currents. Mapping lands previously populated solely by AIs.

Living in this virtual world has also made him a bit odd.

"Twist. What brings you here?" His voice issues from speakers in the labyrinth, coming to me in stereo. Grab is everywhere.

"I just wanted to see how you are doing." The lie tastes sour in my mouth as I perch on the low stool beside his bed.

I'm never sure where to look when I visit Grab. He sees me through a number of cameras, none of which are mounted on his body. So looking at his empty eyes is pointless. And disturbing.

Still, it seems weird not to look at someone while I'm talking to them. My eyes flit around uncertainly, alighting on his shaven scalp, his shrunken throat, the tube filling his mouth. His skin is pasty and sickly looking, like the belly of a cave lizard. I fidget on the stool, scratching at my neck as if I were the one sprouting tubes.

The speakers hum to life. Grab's voice fills the room.

"I am doing so many things I cannot begin to count. While I am talking to you, I am simultaneously having a conversation with an AI on the evolution of Greica's biosphere, and reading a report by one of the original surveyors, and looking down on the five canyons through the eyes of a drone."

"That sounds like a lot to juggle."

"Perhaps." He pauses for a second, the vocal equivalent of a shrug. "I don't really think about it. Every day my mind becomes more comfortable with the expanded capabilities afforded me by my... situation. Multi-tasking has become as natural as breathing."

"Do you like it?"

Static blips through the speakers. Half a second and then it's gone. I can't even begin to guess what it means.

"Like or dislike doesn't enter into the equation. It is interesting. It keeps my mind active and diverted from the sad realities of my flesh. That is enough."

I chew on that. I want Grab to be happy. Dust, I want him to get better so he can be free from these machines.

But it's looking like that's never going to happen. This may be as close to happiness as he can get now. This strange, cyborg creature may be all that's left of my friend from here on.

Something Grab said hits me. "Wait, you're flying over the canyons right now? You have access to the security drones?"

"I can access anything that is connected to the datanet."

"Do you know about the slavers?"

"I know there is an extensive underground slave trade in operation between the cities of the five canyons."

"Do you know who they are? Can you map their tunnels?"

"I know the identities of a number of suspected dealers, yes. As for the tunnels, that is beyond my current capabilities. The drone net is very effective at mapping and monitoring the surface of the canyons. It is significantly less effective at monitoring the tunnels and caves. That is one of the reasons the slavers use them."

I chew my lip, my heart racing with excitement. I didn't realize Grab had become so powerful. He's practically an AI himself. A friendly one. With access to the Guardian's datanet.

My head spins with the possibilities.

"Who are they, Grab? Who are the heads of the slaver operation?"

"Those who move the physical slaves or their investors?"

"The physical slaves. I don't care about the money men."

Static crackles for the space of two breaths, while Grab's mind races through electronic corridors. "There is a triad who control all of the slave trade in and out of Canyon City. Their names are Wei Heng, Amir Hamidu, and Jepet Cotton."

I clench my teeth, hot anger running down my spine. Jepet. It all comes back to Jepet.

"Thanks, Grab. You're amazing." I stand up, energized and ready to charge straight into Jepet's lair alone if I have to.

"You are welcome. Was that all you wished to know?" There is a note of something like hurt in his voice, and I realize he must be lonely in here. I feel guilty for not visiting more. It also reminds me I got so excited about the slavers, I almost forgot to ask about the thing that brought me in here in the first place.

"Can you access the plan for the big assault on the Outsiders?" I struggle to keep my voice casual. "I'm curious what grand strategy our glorious leaders are cooking up."

Grab doesn't answer. I stand there amid the whirring and clicking of his machines, breathing in the hot, stale air. Sweat prickles my neck. I wonder if I've offended him. Or if I've triggered some security flag. Maybe a squad of Guardians is coming to arrest me right now. Maybe Grab is gathering a swarm of drones in the hall outside the door. My breath becomes short, my throat dry.

Then Grab stutters back to life. "That was interesting."

"What was interesting?" I'm poised on my toes, ready to run.

"I've never tried to get into that part of the system before. It took a bit of finesse."

"But you were able to do it?"

"Yes."

"You got the plans for the assault?"

"Yes. I've transferred them to a dataspike for you."

I hear a click, and a dataspike slides out of a slot near my elbow.

I take it with trembling fingers. This is it. My spying for the Outsiders isn't hypothetical anymore. If I turn this data over to them, it's treason. I'll get the cages if they catch me.

I take a deep breath and tuck the spike into my belt.

"Thanks, Grab. And I'm sorry."

"For what?"

For getting you involved in treason.

"For … you know. Everything."

A smile ghosts across his mouth.

"Don't worry about it. I may have lost the use of my body, but I have gained something far better."

I look at the ruin of my friend lying in the bed and run my fingers over the tip of the dataspike.

"I hope you're right."

12

My skin itches as I stride through the halls of the Mesa. I feel eyes on the back of my neck. I do my best to walk naturally, keeping a tight rein on the urge to break into a run.

The dataspike drags on my belt. Heavy with the weight of my guilt.

I'm keenly aware that every person I pass would kill me if they knew what I was carrying. What I intend to do with it.

There's no going back from this. I've officially crossed the line. Whatever happens from now on, I am a traitor. If I get caught, there will be no mercy for me.

The thought is terrifying, but also freeing in a way. I'm not balanced between two worlds anymore. I've taken the leap. I don't know where I'll land, or how things will turn out, but at least I've taken action. The game has been set in motion.

The only problem is: I don't know what to do with the dataspike now that I've got it.

When my dad and Tempest sent me back into Merrimac, they said they'd be in touch when they needed me. They didn't tell me how to get in touch with them. Which means I'm holding information that's vital to their survival, but I have no idea how to deliver it.

Well, that's not entirely true. I do have one idea. It's just not an idea I like.

My stomach churns as I stand in the dust, looking up at the enormous honeycombed complex. The cold wind spins dust devils down the street, and nips at my ears. It smells of frost and the coming winter.

The street is packed with shoppers, but they part smoothly around me, flowing past without jostling. It's something that's been happening ever since I became a Guardian. Even though I've got a loose robe over my armor, they still know. Maybe it's my scarf. Maybe it's the way I stand. Maybe it's something else entirely, some invisible scent coming off me that screams Guardian to the ancient receptors in their hindbrains.

Whatever it is, I don't like it very much. It means I'm marked. In Canyon City, I can never be a part of the crowd again.

Of course, I'm only thinking these thoughts because I'm stalling. I don't want to go in there. Don't want to face the past again.

But I can't think of any other way to get in touch with the Outsiders. I guess sometimes you have to go back to go forward.

Fin is at his usual spot behind the counter when I push open the heavy door to Wayfinders. Multi-lensed glasses on his face. Cobwebs in his grey fringe of hair. Completely absorbed in some project on his workbench. Exactly the way I knew he'd be.

Except he's not at all the person I thought he was. The kindly eccentric who took me in was a facade.

My hands clench into fists. I want to lash out, smash whatever's closest. He lied to me. For years.

I grind my jaw and shudder with the effort of keeping myself under control. I take a deep breath. Then another.

Eventually, I manage to push the anger down. Unclench my jaw enough to speak.

"Fin."

He looks up, his eyes going wide.

"Theo?"

The sound of his voice makes my anger flare, and I have to swallow it down again before I can speak. My words are a strangled croak.

"Yeah. It's me."

"I'm so glad you came back." He gets up from his stool and takes a couple of hesitant steps towards me. He falters when he sees the look on my face.

"I'm not here to forgive you," I say. "I need your help."

His face falls. "Ah. Well. Of course, I'll do whatever I can, Theo."

"I need to get a message to my dad. I assume you have some way to contact him."

He twitches, and his lips purse. I can tell he's trying to decide what he should reveal to me. But I've already read the answer to the only question that matters in his reaction. He knows how to send a message. I just have to convince him to do it.

"It's important, Fin. Life or death kind of important."

Still he hesitates, bushy eyebrows bending downward as he considers. "You don't know how to contact him yourself?"

"No. He only told me to watch and keep my head down. That he'd contact me when the time was right. But this can't wait. I need to get a message to him today."

"That's a tall order. Even if I agree to help you, I can't guarantee he'll get it today. Communication outside the wall isn't what you'd call reliable."

"We have to try. The Guardians are going to launch a massive attack on the Outsiders. They're determined to wipe them out as payback for the governor's assassination. If they don't get this information today, it might be too late."

He frowns, drumming his fingers on the tabletop as he considers my words.

"All right. Give me the information and I'll do my best to see that they get it."

"No, I want to deliver it myself."

"Not possible. You look like a Guardian. The minute they see you coming, they'll disappear like shellbabies. You have to give it to me."

I stare at him, every muscle rigid, frustration surging through me.

He holds my gaze, not backing down. He speaks quietly, like he's trying to soothe a wild animal.

"I've kept your father's secrets for a long time. You have to trust me. I'll do everything in my power to get it there today."

I want to scream and pound things into dust, but I swallow my anger down.

"Fine. But you'd better not fail me again. If you do, I'll bring this place down around your ears."

His mouth opens in shock. Then sadness fills his eyes. He nods heavily.

"I understand."

I hand over the dataspike, turn on my heel, and march out of the shop. I don't look back.

13

____

People jump out of my way as I charge down the street. My face must be murderous.

You would think handing over the dataspike would make me feel better, like I'd done a good thing. But it only makes me feel more desperate. As if things are moving too fast, and I have to run to keep up.

I round a corner and slam into a silver wall.

No, not a wall.

I tilt my head up to meet Knott's grin.

"Going somewhere, Boss?"

"Knott, just the person I was looking for. Where's Shadow?"

She shrugs. "At Southspire, I guess."

"Good. Let's go meet her. I'm in the mood to hit something."

Shadow is standing in the same place we were laying out injured victims just a couple of days ago. The crimson dust has swallowed the bloodstains as if they were never there. She's got a black robe on, her thin armor almost invisible beneath the folds. Still, people give her a wide berth that becomes even wider when Knott and I stride up to join her.

I catch some kids staring at us and think about how we must look to them. Three Guardians in full armor. A full fist of cans, as we used to say when I was their age. If there were any doubt left, the look in their eyes confirms it. I've become the thing I always feared. A strutting soldier, using my armor to get my way.

It gives me pause, but only for a second. Jepet's a bully. Violence is the only language he speaks.

I nod to Shadow. "You sure you want to do this?"

"We're crew, Twist. We've always got your back, no matter what."

"Just wanted to give you an out. This could get messy."

"I hope so." Knott grins and draws her massive warpknife. It hums to life, the edge lined in green light. My skin tingles in response.

Shadow squashes her springy hair down under her helmet. I follow suit, clicking on my com.

"Lead on."

Shadow takes us into a warren of dingy alleys. We pass nondescript doors covered in peeling paint, their outer gates closed and locked. This part of town doesn't like mornings. Those doors will open to reveal bars and gambling dens after dark, full of rowdy laughter. But right now, in the cold early light, they look tired and worn. Stained with the broken dreams of a thousand patrons. Not even the rats are out now.

"Jepet and his guards will still be in bed." Shadow echoes my thoughts. "It's a good time to catch them by surprise."

I grin. I've got a surprise for them all right.

She stops us at the mouth of an alley that winds up into a narrow slot canyon.

"Wait here while I take care of the door guard."

Shadow slips into the dark slot. Knott and I stand and watch our breath steam in the cold morning air. Frost glimmers on the wall beside us.

Knott clears her throat, suddenly awkward. "The monsoon will be here soon, I think."

"Yeah, I guess it will."

"It's good. Water is good."

"If you say so."

Back in Papa Grady's camp, the monsoon was anything but good.

We'd huddle inside our tents, shivering while cold rain bucketed down for weeks, washing away tunnels and creating new ones. Reshaping the soft walls of the scablands hour by hour. Supposedly the landscape changes so much they have to remap the five canyons every year after the monsoon passes.

Finally, Shadow's whisper fills my earcones. "Clear."

I step into the winding slot, and Knott clunks along behind me in her heavy armor. I have to admire Jepet's choice of location. The slot canyon restricts us to walking single file, and it twists and turns so much I can never see more than a couple of meters ahead of me. It's highly defensible space, perfect for blocking or trapping attackers.

But it's all useless if your defenders are asleep.

We find Shadow standing outside a low doorway cut into the side of the canyon. An unconscious guard slumps against the wall at her feet.

"The longer we can keep them asleep, the better. From here we need to move quickly and quietly."

I turn and cock an eyebrow at Knott, who smiles and shrugs. Her power armor is built for strength, not stealth.

Shadow sighs. "Just do your best, ok? I'd rather not have to fight for every meter in there."

There's darkness inside the door, lit only by the faint glow of our warpknives.

"Night vision, Jmini."

"Aye aye, Capitan."

My vision goes green, illuminating Shadow's back. Knott's steps clank softly behind me. We're standing in a small entrance cave five meters across. Dark tunnel mouths beckon from three directions.

I subvocalize carefully. "Which way?"

Shadow sweeps the tunnels with her cannon, reading for signs of life. She points to the one in the center. "I'm guessing this way."

"Do you want me to take point?"

She gives me a withering look. I wince and raise my palm in surrender.

"Sorry. Lead on."

As we progress, the tunnel becomes cleaner, the angles of the floor and walls straight and smooth. Man-made.

"This feels right," I whisper.

"Yes, it does." Shadow pokes her head down a side passage, then returns to the main hall and continues. "Stay alert."

It's utterly dark and silent in the complex. Without my augments, I couldn't see the nose on my face. It's familiar and comforting; like my deep-diver days back in Papa Grady's camp. Ten meters or a thousand meters makes no difference. Once you've left the surface, it all becomes the same.

I find myself relaxing and have to fight the impulse. Stay alert. You're not alone in the deep dark here. This is enemy territory.

Knott helps. The clank of her armor sounds impossibly loud in the stillness, and I flinch every time she takes a step. It's a wonder she hasn't woken up the entire complex by now.

"These boys must be heavy sleepers," I say.

Shadow snorts. "Probably passed out from too much partying last night. This lot doesn't see the light of day until well after noon."

"But why aren't there more guards? Is Jepet really so powerful he only has to post a single door guard?"

"Arrogant is more like it. He can't imagine anyone would have the stones to invade his castle."

I open my mouth to reply, but Shadow jerks her hand up. We freeze. For a long moment, all I can hear is my breath rasping against the inside of my visor.

Shadow's voice is so quiet, I almost think I'm imagining it. "Movement on my scanner. Doorway to the right. Ten meters."

My heart beats faster.

I tighten my grip on my warpknife and take three quick steps, pressing myself to the wall beside the doorway. Knott mirrors me, flanking Shadow's other side.

"Five meters … Three."

A rumpled-looking thug steps through the doorway. He's barefoot and wearing a baggy pair of shorts. His uncovered gut sags over the waistband, but there's plenty of muscle beneath that. There's nothing soft about him.

His eyes widen as he sees Shadow. His mouth opens, preparing to shout.

Knott clamps her forearm around the man's windpipe, lifting him off his feet in a sleeper hold. He struggles, knocking a vase over with the toe of his boot. I wince and lunge, snagging it as it clangs across the floor. Knott holds the man firm though, and the lack of air quickly kills his resistance. In a matter of seconds, the big man hangs limp in her arms.

"Do you think anyone heard that?" I whisper as Knott lays the man down against the wall.

A female voice calls out from down the hallway, a sliver of light bisecting the darkness. "Trag? Is that you?"

Shadow hisses. "There's your answer."

"Spines. Our time is running out." I set the vase next to the limp man, moving toward the far door. "Come on, let's go."

We're only ten meters down the hall when the screaming starts.

Lights pop on. Voices shout.

I see double doors at the end of the hall ahead of us, big metal things engraved with fancy whorls and spirals.

"There! That's got to be Jepet's room." I pound toward them, my footsteps ringing on the stone. Twenty meters. Ten. Five.

Something heavy hits me in the side, knocking me off my feet. I hit the wall hard and bounce, then slam into the floor. I lie there for a second, trying to figure out what just happened. I'm not hurt, my armor did a great job of cushioning the blows, but I'm disoriented and dazed.

I look up and see one of Jepet's thumpers looming over me, brandishing a thick metal pipe. He winds up to hit me again.

A burst of cannon fire takes his face off.

Shadow offers me a hand up, the tube of her cannon still glowing. I take it.

"Thanks," I manage.

The hall behind us is chaos. Knott looms over a handful of partially clothed thumpers, tossing them around like milk blossoms. It's a ridiculous sight: a bunch of dwarfs trying to bring down a giant.

They've got no chance against her power armor. All they're going to do is break their bones.

Shadow yanks on my arm. "Come on. She's got this under control. We've got bigger prey."

The heavy metal doors are locked, but Shadow doesn't even hesitate. Her cannon swings up, burning a hole where the lock used to be. Together, we shove the doors open.

An intricate chandelier hangs from a vaulted ceiling, illuminating fine rugs and an enormous canopy bed. Thick velvet curtains sag from the corners. Sitting up, in the center of the bed, is Jepet.

14

———

"What do you think you're doing?" Jepet trembles, but I can't tell if it's rage or fear.

"Good morning, Jepet." Shadow watches the door while I stroll over to the side of the bed and lift my visor. "We need to talk."

His eyes widen. "You!"

"Yeah, me. I've learned some interesting things about you the past couple of days. We're going to have a nice chat, you and I."

"I'm not telling you anything."

I slam my armored fist into his face, snapping his head back. Blood blooms beneath his nose.

"You little dust-speck. I'll kill you for this." His eyes burn.

"You're welcome to try. But first you're going to tell me what I want to know." I hit him again. It feels good, so I do it a third time.

A part of me is horrified at how casually I'm beating a defenseless man. How natural violence feels to me now.

The rest of me just wants to hit this spine-sucker.

"Where's my sister?"

Jepet slumps against his headboard. Blood sheets down over his chin. His eyes are glassy with pain.

"I don't know what you're…"

I punch him again.

"Wrong answer. Where's my sister?"

"Ask your friend Carlyle." He spits blood at me. It speckles my armor.

"Who's Carlyle?"

He smiles, and his teeth are outlined in blood.

"You're such a stupid little rockhead. Down here assaulting legitimate businessman in their own homes, and you don't even know what you're looking for."

The doors clang open, and a handful of thumpers push into the room. Unlike the first wave, this batch is geared up with armor plating and heavy cannons. A woman with a knife-edged nose leads them.

They open fire.

Cannon blasts punch me in the chest and shoulder, knocking me back into the wall. Cannons aren't going to penetrate my armor, but that doesn't stop the blasts from hurting. I feel like I'm being kicked by giant Horrors.

Shadow and I take cover behind the enormous bed and return fire. The thumpers retreat behind the door frame. Energy lances back and forth, burning holes in the walls, filling the air with dust and smoke.

"Twist!" Shadow's voice is urgent in my earcones. "Behind you!"

I turn to find the bed empty. Beyond the bed gapes an open door that wasn't there before. Jepet is gone.

"Dust storms." I curse and jump to my feet, but cannon fire drives me down again. "Shadow!"

"I've got you. I'll hold the muscle here."

"Are you sure? You're outnumbered five to one."

As the words leave my mouth, Knott looms up behind the thumpers. She grabs one of them and drags him screaming into the hall. Shadow smirks.

"Correction, it's four to two. Don't worry, Twist. Their weapons and armor are no match for ours. We've got this. Go get Jepet."

"All right. Be careful."

"Always. On my mark. Go!"

She lights up the doorway with a sustained burst of fire, forcing the thumpers to pull back.

I roll across the bed and follow Jepet through the secret door.

There's no sign of him in the escape tunnel, but it's a straight shot into the mountain. A hundred meters in, it opens into a natural cave system. I skid to a halt, frantically looking for heat signatures.

"Jmini, any signs of life?"

"A moment, Capitan. Scanning."

Jepet chose his escape route well. This cavern is a maze of stalag-mites, and a dozen tunnel mouths pock the walls. He could have gone anywhere.

"I've got something, Capitan."

A blue map pops up, overlaying my vision. Something moves in the top corner.

"Jepet! Don't make me have to run you down. Give up and I'll go easy on you." My voice bounces around the cavern, echoing back at me from weird angles.

Jepet doesn't respond.

Jmini gives a small cough that sounds suspiciously like a smoth-ered laugh. "Did you really expect that to work?"

"No, but it was worth a try. He might have yelled back and helped us get a fix on him."

"A valid point."

Jepet's trail follows a natural crevice in the rock, though I can see where they've taken hammers and chisels to it, smoothing and flat-tening the floor. It follows a fairly young lava flow, and the walls are jagged, speckled with hardened pockets of air.

I quickly come to a branch and turn right, following the dot on my display. After a few more turns, the dust becomes packed down into a clear trail. A lot of feet have come this way. I wonder if Ianna's were among them.

There are toe prints in the dust, and I imagine slaves coming through here. Barefoot, clad in rags, scared and hungry. Would they be chained? Shackled? Tied together with rope? Or would the slavers herd them along unfettered, secure in the knowledge that the slaves had nowhere to go?

Because they really wouldn't. I bet the slavers would be the only ones with lights, walking at the front of the line. Unlike me, the slaves wouldn't be equipped with nightvision and infrared. To them, the side passages would be filled with impenetrable darkness. Fleeing into that would be madness.

Best case scenario you'd brain yourself on a rock and die instantly. Worst case you'd fall down a crevice and break a leg. Then you'd slowly starve to death, trapped and alone in darkness so thick you can't even see your own nose. Not the most pleasant way to go.

I try not to picture Ianna starving to death in the darkness. Of course as soon as I try not to see it, the image seizes my imagination. My sister, her leg bloody and broken, dirty tear tracks streaking her cheeks. Her eyes are wide with fear, staring into the darkness. Her voice hoarse from screaming.

I lean against the wall of the tunnel, my breath rasping in my throat. I grind my teeth so hard I can hear them cracking.

"Are you all right, Twist? Your heart rate has spiked." Jmini's calm tones pull me out of the vision.

"I'm fine. I just need a minute."

Anger surges within me. I'm a Guardian now, and I still haven't found my sister. What good is all this power if I can't even protect my family?

I slam my armored fist into the wall, spraying shards of rock everywhere. Hitting things seems to be all I'm good for these days.

The anger seeps away, leaving an exhausted hollow feeling in its place. I zero in on the moving blue dot that is Jepet, and lurch back into motion.

15

———

I've been following the slaver's trail for over an hour, the blue dot always ahead of me, barely visible at the edge of the map. Over the last fifteen minutes, the shard in my collarbone has started tingling, then itching. It's worse with every step, no matter how much I scratch the skin around it. It distracts me so much I don't notice the tunnel getting light, until I squeeze through a narrow gap in the rock and step out into a chamber full of stars.

My mouth falls open.

"You've got to be kidding me."

Greicagins. At least a dozen of them, twinkling in the darkness. More than I've ever seen in one place before. A fortune like this could set someone up for life.

"This doesn't make any sense, Jmini. What are these doing here? Why haven't the slavers harvested them?"

"Probably because they don't know they're here."

"What do you mean? We're following the slavers' trail. How could they not know they're here?"

"Actually, you left the slavers' trail about fifteen minutes ago."

"What?"

I turn my eyes to the ground, scanning the dust for footprints.

There's no sign of the well-trodden trail I've been following. There's no sign of any trail at all.

Panic grips my chest. I whirl around and look back the way I came. Nothing but dust and gravel. The only footprints I see are my own.

I check my retinal map. The blue dot of Jepet is still there, blinking in the upper corner. My panic backs off a step. Everything is all right. I haven't lost Jepet.

"Why didn't you tell me I was wandering?"

"You didn't ask." Jmini sounds defensive. "Besides, you seemed like you knew where you were going. I thought you simply wanted to take the road less traveled."

"Great, now we could be lost down here."

"No, Twist, we could not be lost down here. I've mapped every step you've taken since we left the surface. Retracing your steps will be raindrops."

Jmini trying to use slang makes me smile. "Raindrops, huh?"

"All the kids are saying it."

I chuckle. "In the future, please inform me when I stray from a trail I'm following."

"Aye aye, Capitan!"

Checking the blue dot again shows me it hasn't moved. Or if it is moving, it isn't moving very fast. Maybe I have time to catch my breath.

I lower myself onto a rounded boulder and sigh, leaning back against the wall of the cavern. It feels good to take the weight off my feet. Now that I've stopped, I can feel my calves and knees throbbing. How has Jepet stayed ahead of me all this time? He's a barefoot, out-of-shape slaver. It doesn't make any sense.

The tube in the collar of my armor provides water, and I suck in a greedy drink.

"Seriously though, I can't believe you didn't at least mention it when I left the slavers' trail. What were you thinking, Jmini?"

"I thought you were chasing Jepet. Wasn't that the reason we came down here in the first place?"

"Touché. Well, at least we're still tracking him."

I take another drink. My shard itches something fierce, and I scratch around my collarbone intently, digging down beneath my breastplate. Then I stop, thinking of the reddened, bulging flesh beneath the tip of my finger. I remember how my skin used to tingle right before I found a score when I was deep diving. I think about how intense that feeling has been since I got my shard implanted.

"Hey, Jmini? Do shards resonate in the presence of other greicagins?"

There's a two-second pause before he speaks, which lets me know he's searching his database for the answer.

"I find only one reference to such a phenomenon. An essay published by a Captain Steel forty-two years ago."

"Captain Steel? The same Captain Steel who was the hero of the Horror War?"

"The same. Though the paper was published later, nearly a decade after the war ended."

I whistle, impressed. Captain Steel is a legend. I used to pretend to be him when I had stick-battles as a kid.

"What does it say?"

"Nothing important. It was dismissed as nonsense by the scholars of the time."

"Can I read it?"

"If you wish. Though I strongly suspect you will be wasting your time."

"Indulge me, Jmini."

He mimics a long-suffering sigh. "Suit yourself."

The text of the paper pops up on my retinal display.

I can see immediately why it wasn't taken seriously. Captain Steel isn't much of a writer, and he definitely doesn't have a scientific background. Instead of laying out an argument with facts and data to back it up, he rambles, words meandering around the topic with the stream of his thoughts. He sounds like a nut.

Jmini was right. This is garbage.

I'm about to close the paper when a paragraph catches my eye. It talks about how his hand would tingle when he held one greicagin close to another. There's no mention of shards though and I can find nothing else about it in the disorganized text.

Still. Maybe there is something to my theory. But it doesn't explain why my skin would tingle when I was a deep diver, long before I had an implanted shard.

I sigh. Maybe I'm just as crazy as Captain Steel.

Tucking my water tube away, I stand, stretching out the kinks in my back. Time to get moving again. There's no way Jepet can keep this up for much longer.

I check my map and freeze. The blue dot is moving toward me. In fact, it's almost here. I turn to face that direction, scanning the cavern.

Spines. The light from the greicagins is messing up my night vision.

Drawing my warpknife, I squint through the twinkling half-light. The blue dot comes closer. He should be coming into view any second now.

A high-pitched shriek pierces the cavern. I stagger against the wall, clutching my ears.

Jmini triggers my implants, shooting me full of adrenaline. The world slows down, the cavern coming into crystal focus.

A Rock Horror rushes into the cavern, towering over me. Three meters long from eyes to tail. The blue dot of my display blinks squarely in the middle of its torso. It's hard to tell in the uneven light, but its carapace looks white on the sides, with blue running down the back. It's not as big as some of the Horrors I've seen, but that doesn't make it any less terrifying.

As it opens and closes its pincers, I crouch in a defensive stance. It cocks its head, multi-faceted eyes glittering in the greicagin light. There's a wound on its front leg, sky-blue fluid seeping down into the dust.

I don't understand. Did it eat Jepet? Have I been following a Rock Horror all this time?

16

We watch each other. I'm vibrating with tension, my body keyed to full alert. The seconds tick by, and still it doesn't attack. What is it waiting for?

My shard burns. I try to ignore it, but it's becoming painful, like dozens of ants biting at my flesh. I want to scream. Dig the thing out with my warpknife and fling it away.

But I don't dare scratch it. I can't shift my attention away from the Horror. It'll be on me in the blink of an eye.

The colors on its carapace begin to pulse, different areas lightening and darkening in turn. The wounded leg stays dark.

Watching it makes me feel funny. Waves of warmth move over my skin, flowing outward from the shard, and I get the insane feeling the Horror is trying to talk to me.

"Put the warpknife down." The ragged stranger from the wall steps into the cavern, a dark shadow against the greicagin glow.

"You're dust-crazy. That thing will tear me apart."

"No, it won't. It's just as scared as you are. Trust me. Put the warp-knife down."

The Horror cocks its head. I feel a question cross my skin. My eye goes back to the seeping wound on its leg.

Despite everything I've been told about Horrors, I can feel the truth of the stranger's words. The creature is scared too.

Is this really happening? Am I losing my mind?

I remember the stranger's words from the wall, *"What if the Horrors are the key to everything?"*

My warpknife wavers in my hand.

"I don't understand. If the Horrors are intelligent, why are humans on Greica at all? Wouldn't the first scientific expedition have reported it?"

"Why do humans do anything? Why did we come to Greica in the first place?"

"I don't know. Knowledge? Exploration?"

The stranger snorts. "Guess again."

The sparkling walls of the cavern shine the truth at me.

"Greicagins. They did it so they could mine greicagins."

The realization takes my breath away. The IEC knew the Horrors were intelligent. They covered it up so they could build Canyon City. So they could mine greicagins.

The stranger is right. Humans have killed enough of these creatures.

I gather my resolve and turn my attention back to the looming Horror.

"Can you understand me? I think you're trying to communicate. Don't do anything stupid and neither of us has to get hurt, OK?" I swallow and force the next words out. "I'm going to put down my warpknife now. I'd appreciate it if you'd lower those pincers too." I try to keep my voice calm and level. Soothing.

"I don't think dropping your warpknife is a good idea, Twist." Jmini's voice is barely a whisper in my ear. "That thing could be on you in half a second."

"It's hurt, Jmini. I don't think it wants to fight. You've got to give something to get something, Jmini. Show trust to get trust." I subvocalize carefully, never taking my eyes off the Horror.

"Show insanity to get madness?"

"Shut up, Jmini. I'm trying to concentrate."

Out loud, I say, "I'm going to lower my warpknife on the count of three. One. Two."

My hands are shaking. Jmini's right, this is crazy. If I'm wrong, that thing will tear me apart in seconds.

No. The Horrors are the original Outsiders. They were the first to be exploited and killed by the IEC's greed.

I won't participate in genocide anymore.

"Three."

I lower the warpknife to my side and force my posture to relax, slowly coming up out of my fighting crouch. I hope the Horror can't sense how hard my heart is hammering in my chest. I clip the warpknife onto my belt and turn my empty palms up before me.

"There. I put down my weapon. Now you put down yours."

The Horror stands motionless, frozen in time. Even the colors pulsing on its carapace have stilled. I've stopped breathing. My heart is in my throat.

My hands really want to go back to the hilt of my warpknife. Keeping them extended and empty is the hardest thing I've ever done. Sweat slides down the back of my neck. The moment stretches forever.

Then the Horror pulses once, blue moving into white across its back. Its eyes glitter. The shard in my collarbone pulses in response, warmth rippling over my chest in a wave.

It cocks its head, opening and closing its pincers. Then it abruptly lowers them to its side. Some emotion I can't identify shivers through my shard.

"That's it. We're on the same side. No need to fight each other." The stranger's voice is calm and soothing.

Relief makes my knees weak, but curiosity keeps me on my feet. I can't tear my eyes away from the shifting colors of the Horror's carapace.

"What's your connection to my shard?" I ask. "Why can I feel you through it? Can you feel me too?"

I try pushing a thought through the shard. I focus on a simple question.

The Horror doesn't react, and I don't feel any pulses of communication flowing through me.

No. That's not entirely true.

I do feel something, it's just very weak. The tiniest hint of something rippling across my chest.

Maybe I'm too weak to communicate with it.

Or maybe I'm just too far away.

"Do you want me to look at your leg? I've got some spray bandage that'll seal that cut up for you."

I slowly pull the spray vial off my belt and step toward the creature, keeping my palms extended. It seems bigger up close, the top of its back looming above my forehead. It watches me carefully, multifaceted eyes glittering.

I take another slow step and extend the vial toward the blue and white carapace. I hit the spray button.

Suddenly the Horror is pivoting, swinging its pincers down at my head. I scream and throw my arms up in a desperate block, knowing it will be useless. The pincer slams against my shoulder, knocking me to the ground.

I cower, waiting for the final blow.

It never comes.

The Horror skitters away into the darkness.

I sag against the ground, lightheaded, as if all the air has rushed out of the room. I lie there, weak as an exposed shellbaby, feeling my lungs fluttering inside my ribcage, my pulse pounding against the side of my neck.

Jmini whistles softly. "Apparently it doesn't like to be touched."

My mouth is so dry it takes me three tries to work up the saliva to respond.

"Let's not do that again."

"You don't have to ask me twice. Can we leave this place now?"

I check my retinal display. No blue dots anywhere. The stranger is gone. Wherever Jepet ran off to, it's not here.

"Dust storms. All that for nothing. Take me home, Jmini."

I lever myself up off the ground, holding onto the wall until the cavern stops spinning. I feel like I've just run fifty kilometers in full armor.

"Plotting a course for home, Capitan."

17

Getting out of the caves takes just as long as getting in did. After all that, the last thing I want to do is walk more. So naturally our squad is assigned to perimeter patrol.

"Cheer up, it could be worse, Twist."

Shadow scuffs the dust twenty meters to my left. Knott clanks along on my other side. We're walking a section of canyon the Outsiders used to ambush a caravan a few days ago. Cliffs thousands of meters tall loom on both sides of us, layered with red and white strata. Reaper plants cluster in hollows, spiny limbs snaking out like fingers. A desert dasher zips across the open ground in front of us, kicking up a trail of dust. Its little legs are a blur.

Drones would be a more effective patrol, but less impressive. Command thinks that a feet-on-the-ground presence is more of a deterrent.

As if my feet haven't covered enough ground today.

"How could it be worse, Shadow?"

"Rory could be out here with us."

That pulls a laugh out of me. "You're right. That would definitely be worse."

"I do not know. I miss him sometimes." Knott surprises us both. "He was a spine in the bottom, but he was our spine in the bottom."

"Yeah, and that spine definitely got into our bottoms at the end." Shadow chuckles. "I know what you mean, though. He was good at keeping the squad loose. It's still hard to believe he betrayed us like that. I blame Twist."

"Me? What did I do?"

"I think we'd need to ask Kass about that."

I feel my face grow warm inside my helmet. I'm glad I've got my visor down.

"Kass was only an excuse," Knott says. "Rory would be Rory no matter what."

"Truer words were never spoken, Knott." I turn my head, scanning the cliffs to my left. Despite the bright sun, patches of ice glint where a pair of water collectors tail down into the shade at the base of the cliff. Dozens of cave mouths gape back at me. My dad's in there somewhere. He could be watching us right now, for all I know. "How's little Sami doing?"

"Better. I got anti-virals from the Mesa. He perked up quick."

"Ah, the joys of being part of the ruling class," Shadow says.

"It is better to let my brother be sick?" I can feel Knott's frown.

"No, of course not. What's the use of being a Guardian if you can't help your family? For those of you that have families, that is. Me, I just get to pamper myself."

"What about your new girlfriend, don't you pamper her?" I watch Shadow stumble at my words. "What, you thought we didn't know?"

"She's not my girlfriend." Her voice sounds strained. "We're just friends."

"Uh-huh. Pretty good friends, from the look of it. I saw you holding hands in the market the other day."

"Mind your own business, Twist."

My helmet rings like a gong as she bounces a rock off the side of my head. I laugh.

Shadow changes the subject.

"So how did you really escape that Horror this morning?"

"I told you. I put down my warpknife and it put down its pincers. I communicated with it."

"Through the shard in your collarbone."

"That's what it seemed like, yes."

I can feel Shadow roll her eyes.

"And then Captain Steel and Heda Dustorm rode up in a cloud of dust."

I grimace. This is Canyon City's version of, "And they lived happily ever after." People say it when they think you're full of dust.

"And they killed twenty Horrors with a single blow."

"Fine, don't believe me."

"Come on, Twist. If we could communicate with the Horrors, why would we have spent the past hundred years fighting them?"

"I don't know, Shadow. I wasn't alive for the past hundred years, was I?"

"I just mean somebody else would have figured it out a long time ago. I think you got lucky. The Horror you found wasn't hungry or something."

"I know what I felt."

"In your shard."

"Yes."

"That tingles when you get near greicagins. Including when you draw your warpknife."

"Yes!"

"Knott, does your shard tingle?"

"No."

"Neither does mine. I'm sorry, Twist, but your story doesn't stack up."

"I know it sounds dust-crazy. But I know what happened to me."

Shadow sighs. "Speaking of families, did you get anything useful out of Jepet before he escaped?"

"No. All I got out of him was the name of someone named Carlyle."

"Carlyle?" Shadow sounds like she's choking. "Are you sure you got that name right?"

"Yeah, why? Who's Carlyle?"

"Oh, this is too good. I can't believe you don't know who the Carlyles are."

Her superior tone irritates me. "I'm sorry I don't know everything. Are you going to tell me who they are, or are you just going to laugh at me?"

"Sorry, Twist. I wasn't laughing at you. I just … well, you'll understand in a minute." She pauses, and her voice becomes quiet and serious. "As far as I know, there is only one Carlyle family in Canyon City. And if they're involved with the slavers, we are in way over our heads with this."

She pauses again and I grind my teeth, willing her to get on with it.

"You remember your friends Julius and Octav?"

"Big, blond, insufferably superior twins? One that I killed and one who hates me? How could I forget? What about them?"

"Their last name is Carlyle."

18

———

I hurry down the dust-choked streets, staring up at the Mesa as I push people out of my way. I earn more than a few hostile glares, but by the time their eyes catch up to me I'm already half a block away. I haven't got time for them. I'm focused on one thing, and one thing only: Sunrise, shining like a jewel atop the Mesa.

Even though I'm a Guardian now, I've never been up there. My assignments always take me outside the city, not to its heart. Even though I'm no longer part of the great unwashed masses, Sunrise feels as distant as ever. A symbol of everything I'll never be, no matter how many Guardian Tournaments I win.

As I approach the base of the spire, I wonder if they'll even let me in. Just because I'm a Guardian doesn't mean I can go anywhere I want. Technically, they have no reason to deny me, but the real world doesn't run on technicalities. I think I got that backwards, actually. Sometimes I feel like the world is nothing but technicalities.

"Twist, don't do this." Shadow grabs my arm, dragging me to a halt. Knott comes pounding up behind her.

"Let me go!" I yank my arm away, but Knott grabs my other arm. I glare up at her. "I've finally got a decent lead on my sister. Nothing is going to stop me from checking it out."

"OK, but just stop and think, Twist. Assuming you can even get into the Carlyle estate, what are you going to do when you get there?"

"I don't know. Poke around until something comes loose."

"Don't you see how counter-productive that is? There are better ways of getting information. Let me ask around and see what I can find out."

"It's too slow, Shadow! Every second I stand here, something awful could be happening to my sister. I'm not waiting any longer!" It takes all my strength, but I wrench my arm away from Knott.

Shadow puts a hand on the big girl's shoulder. "Let him go, Knott. When he gets arrested, we'll be here to bail him out."

I take off at a run. Let them try to arrest me. I've been waiting three years for this day. Now is the time to act.

In the lift at the base of the Mesa I hesitate, my finger poised over the top floor. Pressing it makes me feel like I did as a boy, sneaking into the Quarry at night to watch the duels. Like I'm doing something forbidden.

"You're a Guardian. You can do this."

I take a deep breath and press the button. The car begins to rise.

"Are you sure you don't want to change first?" Jmini's voice startles me. "Put on your dress uniform, perhaps?"

I look down at my dusty armor. Maybe Jmini's right. The guards will never let a dirty rockhead like me in the gates. What was I thinking?

But I'm so close. My years of searching might finally be at an end. Can I bear to put it off for half an hour while I get cleaned up?

Before I can make up my mind, the door slides open, filling the car with fresh air and sunlight. I step out, squinting against the glare, wind pushing at my chest. The sky opens above me, blue streaked with brush-stroke wisps of clouds, free of the canyon walls.

My knees go weak and I sway, looking up at all that open space. How do people live here? I feel like the wind is going to carry me off into that endless sky.

It takes an effort of will to tear my eyes away from the heavens. I clamp my jaw tight and set my eyes on the gate.

Sunrise isn't bounded by a wall, it's bounded by the sheer sides of the Mesa, falling away in all directions. Up here, it's literally possible to walk off the edge of the world. As kids we used to watch for falling bodies, convinced the wind could hurl people around like dust. We never saw one, but that didn't stop us believing.

Maybe Sunrisers have a similar belief when it comes to gates. They believe the gate will stop anyone who tries to come into Sunrise, despite the fact that there is no wall accompanying it. As far as I can tell, any hypothetical invaders could simply walk around the gate in a dozen steps.

I approach the gate like a good soldier. I'm not a dirty rockhead sneaking through crevices anymore. Now I enter through the front door.

The guards in the gatehouse aren't anyone I recognize. No surprise there. There are thousands of Guardians, and I'll probably never meet most of them. Besides, I'm still a rookie. To get a cushy post like this, these guys have probably got seniority.

I revise my opinion as I step up to the window. The pudgy-faced boy and petite girl on duty don't look much older than I am. They are unmistakably Sunrisers, however, their skin suffused with the healthy bronze that everyone up here seems to be born with. Not seniority then. Political connections. Someone in their family pulling strings to keep them as far from combat as possible.

The boy eyes my dirty armor with disdain. "Are you lost, dusty?"

I open my mouth and close it again. In my mad dash to get here, I didn't think about this part. What do I say? That I'm looking for my sister who might be a slave? That I'm planning on charging up to the estate of one of the most respected families in Canyon City to demand answers? I decide to go with a slightly more diluted version of the truth.

"I'm looking for a girl."

"You and me both."

The pudgy kid leers. Behind him, the girl wrinkles her nose in disgust.

"I have good information that she's been sighted at the Carlyle estate," I continue. "If you could just tell me where that is?"

"Do you have an appointment?" The girl's voice makes it clear she knows I don't.

"No. I thought I'd drop by and surprise them."

"You can't do that." The boy puffs with self-importance as he steps closer to the window, blocking the girl with his bulk. He pulls out a datapad. On the screen I see a tiny map of Sunrise, each house labeled with blue text. "You'll need to make an appointment."

I try to make my gritted teeth look like a smile. "How about right now? Do you have an appointment for right now?"

The boy laughs in my face.

"The Carlyles are very busy. The soonest I can get you an appointment is." He consults the pad. "Next week."

"That's ok, I think I'd rather surprise them." I turn and stride through the gate.

"But you can't … Hey! Come back here!"

I ignore the boy's blustering. I've already got all the information I need.

19

"Did you get a look at that map, Jmini?"

"Does the wind blow in the canyons?" Jmini huffs. "What a ridiculous question."

I grin.

"I knew I could count on you. So where am I going?"

A map pops up on my retina display, the route traced in blue.

"That girl at the gate is reporting you."

"Do I look like I care?"

"No, you look like something flitbats have been rolling in the dust."

"I don't have time to play their bureaucratic games, Jmini. I've finally got a good lead on Ianna. I'm not waiting any longer."

Sunrise is a strange place, not at all like Canyon City. For one thing the streets are straight, instead of winding between pillars of stone. They run in wide, flat avenues, paved with cobblestones. For another, and this is probably the weirdest thing, the buildings aren't built inside of stone spires. They sit on the surface, vulnerable to the elements on all sides. Big glass windows cover the walls, making them seem even more exposed. I can't believe people actually live in those things. They look like they're waiting for a good dust storm to blow them all away.

There's nobody else around, which seems odd. The streets of

Canyon City are always bustling. You can find solitude in some of the back alleys, but you have to work at it. Here, I'm striding down what I assume is the main thoroughfare, a street three times as wide as the widest street in Canyon City, and I'm the only soul on it. It feels eerie, like someone has taken all the people away somewhere, and I'm moving through an abandoned world. A ghost town.

That illusion is shattered when I get to the Carlyle estate. A wrought-iron fence runs along the street, all swooping curls and spirals. Behind it, grounds-keepers move through manicured gardens. I scan their faces as I pass, but none of them look like Ianna. The carefully trimmed bushes and rows of blooming flowers fill the air with soft, unfamiliar scents. Where do they get the water for all those plants?

A steward comes running out of the house as I approach the gates. He's wearing a black jacket with long tails that flap in the wind as he runs. He gets to the gate just as I'm pushing it open.

"Can I help you, sir?" he puffs, politely putting himself between me and the house. His cheeks are flushed and sweat beads on his bald pate.

"I'm looking for a girl."

No point in blowing words in the wind. This man is as likely to know if my sister is here as anyone.

"I'm sorry, but Mr. Carlyle isn't at home right now," he says. "Perhaps you could come back another time?"

I stare at him coldly. "No, I don't think I can. You can help me, though."

"Well, that's certainly possible, but Mr. Carlyle would never allow it."

"Then it's a good thing he's not home." I push past him and stride down the path toward the house, forcing him to scamper to keep up with me.

"Sir, please. This is most irregular. I really think you should come back another time."

"And I've told you I can't." I stop and give him my most menacing stare. "You can either help me or get out of my way. But you're not going to keep me from going in there."

His face is so pale, he looks like he's about to faint. He licks his lips nervously, running his eyes over my dusty armor. I can see him turning options over in his head. He doesn't like any of them.

Finally, he swallows and nods stiffly. "Very well. Since it seems you'll be going in no matter what I say, I might as well act as your escort."

I step onto a wide porch that wraps around the house. A couple of chairs and a table are set up to one side. A porch swing sways gently in the breeze. A vase full of yellow cut flowers sits upon the table.

"What's that for?"

The steward looks confused. "For? It's for sitting, sir. Drinking tea out in the fresh air."

I turn to look back at the gardens and imagine people sitting here. Watching the gardeners work while they sit and drink tea. I grind my teeth together, biting back the anger.

"The girl I'm looking for would have been a slave," I tell him. "Brought here about three years ago. Her name is Ianna."

The steward looks startled for a moment, then his professional mask covers it.

"Slaves, sir? I'm sure I don't have the slightest idea what you're talking about. There are no slaves here."

"Don't blow dust at me." I draw myself up as I step closer. We're about the same height, but I do my best to tower over him. Judging from the way he shrinks back, the attempt is a success.

"Well, I suppose someone could have been a slave before they came to the estate. We don't know the full histories of all our workers. It's possible."

"All right, now that we've established that, what about this girl, Ianna? She would have been about twelve at the time. Skinny with curly brown hair."

"I'm sorry, but I wasn't here three years ago, sir. I'm afraid I have no idea." I clench my fists and step forward. He shrinks back, speaking quickly, "I can take you to Mrs. Slate, though. She's in charge of the girls. If anyone would know, it would be her."

"Wonderful. After you." I sweep my hand toward the front door.

Inside, the house is even more unbelievable than it was outside.

Polished stone tiles stretch the length of the hallway, beautifully cut cross sections swirling with reds and whites. Art covers the walls, ranging from tiny things the width of my hand to a life-sized portrait of a man sitting on a boulder at the edge of the Sunrise plateau, magnificently framed by a pink sunset blazing over the scablands behind him. He looks familiar, but I can't quite place his face.

Most unbelievable of all, there isn't a speck of dust anywhere. The Carlyle house is the most immaculate place I've ever seen.

I suddenly feel self-conscious in my grubby breastplate. I wince as I notice my boots tracking dirt onto the tiles as we pass.

"Ah, should I … take off my boots?"

The steward casts me a puzzled look, then comprehension dawns on him.

"Oh, no sir. Don't worry. It will be taken care of." He gives a significant look behind me.

I turn and see a girl with a broom. She's wearing a blue dress with a white apron that looks like some kind of uniform. As I watch, she deftly scoops up my trail of dust. She looks about twelve. The age Ianna would have been when she came here.

I try to picture my sister in a similar uniform, with a similar white kerchief upon her head. I can't do it. Ianna was the type of girl who always had one shoe untied and a pocketful of plakbeetles. Picturing her in such a clean, pressed uniform is beyond me.

"Why don't you use bots? Wouldn't it be more efficient?"

The steward gives me a withering look. "Nobody uses bots these days, sir. The best people all prefer the human touch."

I nod in understanding. Servants are a status symbol up here. Apparently the more real live people you have sweeping your dust, the more important you are. Judging from the number of gardeners and maids I've seen already, the Carlyles must think they're extremely important.

The steward leads me down a long corridor, into another wing of the house. I can't believe how many rooms this place has. It seems to go on forever.

"How many people live here?"

"Just three, sir."

I feel my mouth fall open but can't do anything about it. Three people. This place is almost as big as the mesa Wayfinders is in, and that place holds dozens of shops. This is just one house. For three people. I struggle to wrap my brain around it.

"Why?"

"I'm sorry, sir? Why what?"

"Why all this?" I gesture vaguely around me. "For three people. What do they do with all these rooms?"

The steward's lip curls in scorn. He turns his back on me. "This way, sir."

We find Mrs. Slate seated behind a worn desk in the cellar. She's a sturdy woman, with hair the color of her last name pulled back in a tight bun. Her office is about the size of my bedroom back in the barracks, barely big enough for a desk and a couple of chairs. A big board on the wall contains a list of names and tasks. There are at least fifty names on it.

"Mrs. Slate, this gentleman would like to ask you a few questions." The steward bows and leaves us, his back stiff with disapproval.

Mrs. Slate eyes me warily. She doesn't look impressed, but she doesn't look like she has a stick up her backside like the steward either. She looks like a competent woman, solid and hard working. The kind of woman who holds everything together.

"I'll bet you tracked dust all over my floors, didn't you?" It's not a question, and I turn my eyes down sheepishly. "Well don't just stand there. What can I do for an illustrious member of the Guardians? You are a Guardian, aren't you?"

"Yes ma'am." I bring my eyes up to hers, back on solid footing now. "I'm looking for a girl."

"Well we've got plenty of those." She gestures to the big board on the wall. "Take your pick."

"A specific girl. She would have arrived about three years ago. Her name is Ianna. Ianna Maro."

Recognition flickers in her eyes. "And what would you want with this girl?"

"She's my sister."

Mrs. Slate's face remains neutral.

"I may remember that name," she says carefully. "I'll have to check to see if she's still here."

She's obviously stalling. I'm sure she could recite every name on the duty board without looking at it.

"Don't lie to me," I growl, leaning down over her desk. "Is she here or not?"

"There you are," a familiar voice cuts in behind me.

I whirl around to find a squad of Guardians filling the hall beyond the office door. Ghengis and Rory stand at the front, the visors retracted on their helmets. They sneer when they see me.

Standing at the head of the squad is a ghost from beyond the grave. Octav, his grey eyes flashing beneath perfectly combed ash-blond hair. My breath freezes in my throat.

Then the moment passes, and I remember it's not Octav at all. It's his brother Julius, the one being groomed to be the next governor. Octav is buried in the dust where I put him.

Julius does not look amused.

"What are you doing in my home?" His eyes burn as they take in my scratched breastplate and dusty boots.

"Official business. Nothing you need concern yourself with."

"You have no official business in my home," he spits, not buying my bluff for a second. "Sargent, remove this man at once."

"Yes, sir. I'm going to have to ask you to come with us." Ghengis steps forward, an ugly smile stretching his lips. He cracks his knuckles. "I really hope you're thinking of resisting."

I am thinking about it, but I know it's a futile thought. All I'd accomplish is getting my head kicked in.

Inside, I'm seething. I was so close to getting answers. Five more minutes and I might have found my sister at last. I clamp my teeth shut to keep myself from begging for another minute with Mrs. Slate. It won't do any good, and it'll only give Ghengis the excuse he's looking for.

"Fine. Lead the way." I step out of the tiny office.

Hands grab me by the shoulders and spin me around, wrenching my arms behind my back. My face is shoved into the wall.

"It's not that simple, Twisty." Rory's voice is so low he's practically whispering in my ear.

"Theo Maro." Julius pronounces the words with great gravity, but I can hear the barely concealed glee beneath them. "You are hereby charged with treason."

20

The world drops out from under me. Treason?

Spines. They must know about the dataspike I smuggled to the Outsiders.

I break out in a cold sweat. It's all I can do to keep from thrashing in Rory's grip and attempting to run.

But that would just give them an excuse to rough me up. Instead, I stand straight and look Julius in the eye.

"I could call you out to the dueling grounds for such slander."

"I wish you would." His grey eyes glint with malice.

I stare him down for a long moment, considering the odds. They're not good. If he's anything like his brother, he'd cut me to pieces in a duel.

I think about trying to fight my way out, but there are six of them, and these guys all have the same training and physical enhancements I do.

Even if I managed to run, I wouldn't get far. And running would be an admission of guilt. It's better to go along with them and see what they know. Maybe things aren't as grim as I think.

And maybe the scablands will bloom like the Carlyles' garden.

"Hand over your warpknife," Ghengis orders.

"Fine." I sigh and make a big show of being annoyed by the whole procedure. "But when this misunderstanding gets cleared up, I'm going to expect an apology. I was in the middle of something important here."

That much is true. I stare mournfully at the Carlyle estate as they load me into the back of the transport. Is Ianna in there? Did I get this close only to fail?

I'm more annoyed at that than anything else. If I was going to get arrested, it would have been nice to at least see my sister first. I try to picture her grown up, imagine how her face might have changed as she got bigger. I fail utterly. All my imagination gives me is her eleven-year-old face incongruously set atop a taller teenage body.

They handcuff my wrist to the side of the transport and pile in. Ghengis sits on one side of me, Rory directly across. I stare into Rory's eyes, refusing to look away. I'm not going to give him the satisfaction of looking guilty.

Rory smiles, his brown eyes steady above a field of freckles. He still wears his clay-colored hair cropped close like he did in school, and he's put on a few kilos of muscle. He looks smug, like some obnoxious middle manager with a high opinion of himself. I want to punch him in his smirking mouth.

"Looks like you finally crossed the line, Twisty. I've been waiting for this day."

"Not everyone is content to be a toady like you."

"You always thought you were so special. How's that working out for you?"

"Just because you like being a wart on Ghengis's butt doesn't mean everyone would be. I mean, Ghengis hardly bathes."

I don't even see the elbow coming, I just feel it crack into my teeth, snapping my head back against the side of the transport. The sound of my skull slamming into the metal wall is like a bomb going off in the enclosed space.

"Shut up," Ghengis growls.

I wince against the ringing in my ears and count my teeth with my tongue. It seems like they're all still there. Lucky. I decide to keep my mouth shut. Across the way, Rory grins.

Down in the base, they replace my armor with a shapeless grey jumpsuit. Then they deposit me in a cell and walk away.

I call out to their retreating backs. "That's it? Isn't anyone going to tell me why I'm here?"

Rory answers as he disappears around the corner.

"Relax, Twisty. You've got all the time in the world. Take it slow."

The cell block smells like piss and sour sweat. Three-quarter cubes with smooth walls and bars across the front. A seatless toilet by the wall. A button that makes a narrow bed slide out. Or maybe it's only meant to be a bench. Whatever it is, I'm too wound up to sit on it right now. If I don't move, I'll burst.

I pace the length of my cell like a caged animal. Three steps, turn. Three steps, turn. Back and forth, back and forth. I always wondered why animals did that. Now I know.

On the way in, I saw other prisoners in the cells around me. Vague, huddled shapes in grey jumpsuits. I can't see them through the walls, but I hear them moving around. One sings to herself, a low, mournful lullaby. Are they common criminals? Guardians who didn't follow orders? Outsiders? Or are they traitors like me?

That thought fills me with panic. I've failed everyone. My dad, the Outsiders, Ianna. Everyone I ever cared about. How did I end up in here? What do they know?

The waiting is killing me. Why don't they come question me? At least then I'll know what they know.

Hours pass, and still they don't come. At some point the lights go out. I keep pacing in the dark.

I eventually wear myself out. I'm lying on my side on the bench/bed staring into the dark, when the lights come on without warning. I groan, squinting in the sudden glare. I hear the other prisoners complaining as well.

The sound of a door opening echoes down the hall. Booted footsteps approach.

Adrenaline shoots through me. I swing my feet back down to the floor, every nerve tingling on high alert. I watch the space through the bars.

A pair of Guardians I don't know come into my cell and shove my face against the wall. They wrench my arms behind my back and snap cuffs on my wrists before marching me down the hall to an empty room. They handcuff me to a chair and leave me there, blinking in the overhead light.

Time passes. I stare at the white walls, the cracks in the tiles. The stone is cold against my bare feet. My wrists start to ache where the cuffs cut into my skin.

I wonder where I slipped up. How they knew.

I hope I haven't incriminated anyone else. Grab. Fin. Kass. Shadow and Knott. They could all get swept up in the investigation. I wonder how many lives my treachery will ruin.

The door swings open and Castle strides into the room, with Ghengis and Julius right behind him. He looks at me with disgust.

"Why did you do it?"

I meet his cold blue eyes, trying to look innocent. I don't know if I succeed. "Do what?"

"Don't play dumb. We know everything. This will be easier for everyone if you tell us the truth."

Interesting. He's speaking in generalities, trying to get me to fill in the specifics. A tiny surge of hope shoots up my spine. Maybe they don't know everything after all.

"I don't know what you're talking about, Commandant. No one has told me why I'm here."

His eyes narrow. "Don't play dumb, son. You know we'll get what we want eventually. We can do this the easy way, or we can do it the hard way. Your choice."

My choice. That's funny. As if I had a choice in any of this.

The Outsiders needed my help. My dad needed my help. All of Canyon City did, really. We've all been suffering for the IEC's greed.

I guess some people could have done nothing. Kept their heads down and pretended they didn't know what was happening. Walked away.

But I guess I'm more like my dad. When you know the right thing to do, you have to do it—no matter the cost.

Castle hasn't convinced me he knows anything, though. He's still trying to get me to offer up information for free. I'm insulted if he thinks I'm that dumb.

I say nothing.

Ghengis steps forward and punches me in the stomach. It feels like a cannon blast. I curl forward around the pain, gasping for breath.

He hits me a few more times, for sport, but he doesn't really need to. I'm still trying to recover from that first punch. I think he cracked a rib.

"Why were you at the Carlyles' house?" Castle asks.

I look up at him, my brow creased with confusion. The Carlyle's house? What does that have to do with anything? "I was looking for someone."

"Who?"

I turn the question over in my mind, considering. Could it hurt Ianna somehow if I say I was looking for her? I don't see why it would. Whether she's actually there or not, my looking for her is legitimate family business. I decide to tell the truth and see where it goes.

"My sister."

"Your sister," Julius sneers. "And what would your sister be doing in my house?"

I scowl up into his grey eyes. Now that I've seen his estate, his ridiculously large house with its dozens of servants, I hate him even more. Why does he get to live like that while the rest of us crawl around in the dust?

"Working. Not that you would know what work is."

Julius looks at me in confusion for a moment, then he bursts out laughing. "Are you saying your sister is one of my servants? Oh, that's simply perfect. I couldn't illustrate what a low-born worm you are better if I tried."

"Take these cuffs off and we'll see who the worm is," I snarl.

He laughs at me. "As if I'd lower myself to your level. I'm going to be the next governor of this colony. Can you imagine the governor dueling a common rockhead? It's absurd."

"Is that what I'm here for?" I turn my eyes back to Castle. "Searching for my own sister? I didn't realize simply walking into Sunrise was treason."

Castle studies me for a moment, shadows gathering in the deep cracks at the corners of his eyes. He's never liked me, but in his way he's always been honorable. I'm surprised to see him functioning as Julius's lap dog.

"No, it's not. I would strongly encourage you not to bother our more prominent citizens in their homes, but I'd hardly call it treason." His mouth presses into a thin line, his eyes going hard and cold. "But there are other things going on with you. Things that don't add up. You've been seen consorting with criminals. Care to explain that?"

"I've been trying to find my sister."

Castle shakes his head sadly, like a disappointed father. "No. There's something else. Hit him."

Ghengis does, his heavy fists slamming into my body again and again. By the time he stops I'm slumped forward against my handcuffs, blood dripping from my nose. One of my eyes is swollen shut. I hurt all over.

Castle squats down into my field of view.

"Now. Do you want to tell me a better story?"

21

I awake to someone standing outside my cell. They don't make any sound, but I know they're there. I'm instantly alert, but I keep my eyes shut, listening, waiting to see what they will do.

"I know you're awake, Twist. I saw you twitch when I walked in."

I roll over and open the one eye that's not swollen shut. "Hello, Shadow."

She stands with her fingers wrapped around the bars, forehead pressed between them. She's got bags under her eyes and worry lines at the corners of her mouth. She seems older than I've ever seen her. Still, she smiles when she sees my eye open.

"You look like lizard tails caught in a rockslide."

I chuckle, but the pain in my ribs steals my breath and turns it into a groan. "You should see the other guy."

"I did. Ghengis looked fine to me. Not a scratch on him."

"But mentally, he's a wasteland," I say, tapping my temple.

She snorts. "He's always been a wasteland mentally."

"Exactly. I've got him right where I want him." I slowly lever myself up to sitting. Something shifts inside me, bringing tears to my eyes. Ghengis definitely broke some ribs. Shadow's eyes go dark with concern.

"Grab sends his regards," she says. "He tried to come visit you, but his drones couldn't open the doors."

"That's a serious design flaw. I assume he's working to fix that problem as we speak."

"Yes, I suppose he is." She sighs and turns the tip of a braid between her fingers. "You should come over here so I can hold your hand."

I raise an eyebrow at that, but something in her face tells me not to question it. So I struggle to my feet and stagger over to the bars, every step stabbing pain through my guts. She takes my hand, slipping a small dataspike into it.

"Grab says if you need to get in touch with him, just close your eyes," she whispers.

"Thank you."

"What happened, Twist? Why have they got you down here?"

"You want the official reason or the real reason?"

"Are you saying they're not the same thing?"

"Are they ever?"

A smile quirks the corner of her mouth. "OK. Tell me."

I sag back down onto my cot. "The official reason is I went up to the Carlyle estate looking for my sister."

"I told you to stay away from there." Shadow shakes her head. "Is your sister really up there?"

"I'm not sure, but it's the best lead I've got," I say, shrugging gingerly.

"So you're going back."

A smile is my only response.

"What's the real reason you're here?"

"Come on, Shadow. It's obvious. I'm here because I killed Octav. Julius is never going to let that go. I don't blame him, really. I'd hold a grudge if someone killed my twin brother."

"You really know how to make friends, Twist."

"What's the old saying? 'Keep your friends close and your enemies closer?' Well, I think I'm doing a pretty good job of that, at least."

Shadow makes a show of turning her head to look around the empty cell block. "I don't see any enemies here."

"I'm in their heads. I've got them right where I want them."

"I think you've got it backward, Twist." She rings the bars with her knuckles, the sound echoing off the stone walls. "They've got you right where they want you."

After she leaves, I slip the spike into the dataport behind my ear and lie back on the cot. I close my eyes. There's a rush, and I feel like I'm being sucked down a cable at a thousand kilometers per hour.

I find myself standing in a large workshop. Bright sunlight streams in through high windows, glinting off tables full of silver machines. Grab stands at the center of it all, whistling. He moves parts through the air with a gesture, assembling and tweaking things without touching them. The tubes and wires that keep him alive are gone. He stands straight and tall, a healthy glow in his cheeks. His eyes sparkle when he looks at me.

"Welcome to my domain."

"I love what you've done with the place."

I realize my ribs don't hurt anymore. I cautiously probe them with my fingers and find them whole. Apparently Grab can manipulate my pain receptors here.

"Thanks, I designed it myself."

He continues working as he talks, picking parts up off the various tables with flicks of his fingers, orchestrating the swirling mass in the air like some mad electronic sorcerer.

"What are you making?" I ask.

"A seeker program."

"That's a program?"

He smiles. It's an easy, natural gesture, nothing like the pained smile he gave me the last time I visited his room. "It's easier if I visualize it like this. More fun too. Duck!"

A chunk of metal the size of a fist flies through the space where my head was.

"This place is really sharp. Why didn't you give me this dataspike before?"

"I didn't have it. I put it together this morning. I hope you don't mind, but there are some other things in there too. Things you might need before long."

"Such as?"

"Oh, just an accelerated healing program and a few other things," he says mysteriously, waggling his fingers at me. "Don't worry. I've got your back."

I think about that for a minute, then it's my turn to shrug. Grab sacrificed himself for the crew during our final exam. He's proved himself as far as I'm concerned.

Of course I have no idea how he'll react when he finds out I'm working with the Outsiders, but that's true of everyone. As long as I'm still on this side of the wall, he's got my trust.

"OK. Thanks, Grab."

"You think your sister is at the Carlyle estate?"

"Yes. How did you know?"

He grins. "I have my ways."

"Do you know if she's really there?"

"Not yet, but I will. That's what I'm working on here. This seeker will infiltrate the estate's system. If there's a record of your sister in there, I'll find it."

Warm gratitude expands within me. "That's amazing. Thank you."

Grab brushes my words aside. "It's nothing, don't mention it. Besides, it's not as if I have anything else to do. I'm happy to have a project."

"Still, it means a lot to me. I really appreciate it."

"All right, don't get all mushy on me." He pauses and cocks his head to the side. "Whoops, looks like I've got company. I'll be in touch."

He crooks his finger, lifting me up into the air like one of his parts. Then he flicks me aside and I'm sucked away as quickly as I arrived.

22

I sleep like a dead thing while Grab's healing routines build tiny triage units in my system. When I wake, I feel a little better. Not completely healed, but at least it doesn't hurt to breathe anymore. A couple more nights like that and I'll be good as new.

Physically, anyway. Mentally I'm spinning like a runaway flywheel.

I can't figure out why they came down on me so hard for visiting the Carlyle estate. I mean, sure, I know Julius has plenty of reasons to hate me. I knocked him out of qualifying for the Guardian Games and killed his brother during the final exam, after all.

But locking me up and working me over for visiting his estate seems a little extreme. There's got to be more to it. Some reason they don't want me poking around.

Something Julius is trying to hide.

Maybe Grab's seeker will find something. I guess he sees everything from his nest of wires and tubes now. Like some mechanical imspider crouched in the center of his web.

Shadow would love that image.

I'm sitting on the edge of my cot, lost in thought, when a familiar voice comes through the bars behind me.

"Nice to see you up and about."

Something squeezes inside my chest.

"Hi, Kass."

"Hello."

She lingers in the doorway to the cellblock, one hand on the frame, like she's not sure if she wants to come in or not. Her eyes are restless butterflies, flitting toward me and away.

"I'm glad to see you up and about," she repeats. "I heard you were in pretty bad shape."

"It was nothing. I've had worse."

"Yes, well. I'm still glad you're OK."

She hasn't moved from the doorway. I feel the distance between us yawning like a canyon. We're balanced on a tightrope of words; one false step could send us plunging into the chasm.

"It's good to see you," I venture cautiously. "Is everything all right?"

She tries to laugh, but it comes out as more of a half-choked sob. "Sure, I'm dandy. My boyfriend gets arrested, I get questioned. Everyday stuff."

"You got questioned?" My voice comes out sharper than I intended.

She flinches and I regret my tone. My anger wasn't meant for her. She finally lifts her eyes to meet mine.

"Of course I got questioned. Did you think I wouldn't? You do something stupid and they assume I must know all about it."

I fight to make my voice gentler. "Did they hurt you?"

"No. They just asked a lot of questions and looked at me like I was lying."

She grinds her teeth as she speaks, jaw muscles bulging in her cheeks. They might not have hurt her, but she's obviously been shaken by the experience.

"I'm sorry." I want to go to her, take her in my arms, but the canyon between us feels too deep. Also, there are bars.

She looks away again. "Everything you do is going to reflect on me, you know. Everyone already thinks I'm crazy for dating a rockhead. Then you go and do things like this." She lifts her hands in exasperation. "I thought you were better than this. That you wanted to leave that all behind. But maybe they're right. Maybe you're just going to drag me down with you."

I want to tell her she's wrong. Say I'd never do anything to hurt her.

But I'd be lying. I am going to disappoint her. I'm working with the Outsiders. If that's not dragging her down into the muck, I don't know what is.

I understand why she didn't visit me sooner. She was right to stay away.

"You're right. We were doomed from the start anyway. A Sunriser girl and a rockhead boy? It was never going to work out. Can you imagine introducing me to your family?" The words are sharp-edged in my throat, cutting me, making me bleed. My voice shakes, but I keep talking, forcing them out. "There are things about me you don't know. Things you don't want to know. It's better if you stay away from me."

I knew this day was coming. From the moment I decided to help the Outsiders, I knew there would be hard choices ahead of me. Friends I'd have to betray.

Knowing doesn't make it any easier.

I sit on the edge of the cot, staring at the cold stone floor. I can see Kass watching me out of the corner of my eye, waiting for me to say something more. There's a fist-sized lump in my throat I keep trying to swallow down. It's making it hard to breathe.

Kass won't cry either. Not in front of me, anyway. Which is good, because I don't know if I could hold my resolve if she did.

Time creeps past.

Kass opens her mouth as if she's going to say something. A part of me desperately wants her to. I want her to tell me I'm wrong, tell me it doesn't have to be this way. Convince me to share all my secrets.

After a moment, she closes it again.

I don't know how long she stands there, watching me watch the floor. It feels like hours. Eventually, Kass sighs and turns away. The big metal door clicks shut behind her.

It's better this way. Sooner or later I'm going to get caught, and what I've been doing will come out. If I care about her, I can't let Kass be anywhere near me when that happens. Better to let her walk away now, while she still can.

23

They leave me in the cell for two days. Nobody else comes to visit me. Thanks to Grab's healing subroutines, I'm as good as new physically. But inside I'm frantic with worry.

What do they need two days for? Are they checking out what I said? Maybe they're trying to make me sweat, see if I'll change my story. And what about Ianna?

I've been pacing the floor so much I'm surprised I haven't worn a track across it. I can't take this anymore. I need answers.

I close my eyes and try to find Grab. Nothing happens. I want to scream.

"Jmini, can you get me to Grab?"

"Aye aye, Capitan."

The sense of traveling is different this time. Less like I'm being sucked down a conduit and more like pushing upstream through thick mud. It takes over a minute to make the connection. When we finally get there, I understand why.

Grab is lying in the center of his web, machines humming all around him. Fluids run through the tubes that keep him alive: red and blue and clear. The room looks different than it did the last time I was here, though I'm not sure exactly what has changed. Maybe it's because I'm looking down at him through a camera mounted over the foot of his bed.

Grab looks terrible. His eye cavities are sunken into his skull, the wires of his visual feed running into bruised hollows of flesh. The skin around the wires is red and angry, his stubbly scalp waxy and yellowish. A thin line of drool hangs from the corner of his open mouth.

"This isn't exactly what I meant, Jmini."

"You would have preferred it if I woke an invalid? That seems rather rude."

Before I can reply, Grab jerks awake, turning his blind head from side to side like he's searching for something. Then he turns his empty eye sockets toward the camera I'm looking through and bares a gap-toothed smile.

"Rather cramped in there, don't you think?" he croaks. "Let's go somewhere a little more comfortable."

Everything loses focus and shifts. I'm traveling again.

Resolution snaps back and we're sitting in a room high up the canyon wall. Enormous windows that still can't contain the sunset over Canyon City. The height makes my head spin, and I have to look away from the window. I focus on the thick carpets beneath my feet instead, woven in fantastic patterns. Persian?

I'm sitting in a soft armchair, a steaming cup of matte on the small table beside me. Grab sits in a similar chair, though the scent tells me his drink is dark coffee. Gone are the tubes, wires, and machines that sustain his life, the sallow skin and sunken eyes. He's the perfect picture of health, his hazel eyes shining as they reflect the sinking rays of the sun. He takes a sip of his coffee and sighs with satisfaction.

"That's better. Sorry you had to see that. One day I hope to leave the meat behind for good."

"Leave the meat behind?"

I blow steam from my matte, cupping the warm mug between my hands.

"I want to become an AI," he says. "Convert my brain into software that can run on any platform."

"You can do that?"

"Well, no one has yet, but I don't see why not. It's just a matter of processing speed and memory."

"What would happen to your body?"

He shrugs. "Recycled, probably. I don't know, and I don't care. It wouldn't be my concern anymore."

He's trying to be cavalier about the whole thing, but I can see in the set of his jaw how badly he wants it to be true. How much he hates being trapped in his wasted body.

I'm not sure what to say, so I sip politely at my matte. It's perfect, sweetened with a dollop of honey and a splash of milk.

"How did you know this is the way I like my matte?"

"Jmini told me."

I frown. "Are you two having conversations behind my back?"

A new avatar materializes in the room, a dapper butler in an ascot and waistcoat. His hair is parted carefully on one side. A curling mustache obscures his upper lip.

"We are always having a conversation behind your back, Twist," Jmini's avatar says. "You can't blame us, really. No offense, but our processing speeds are much faster than yours. We can have an entire conversation in the space between sentences."

My mouth is hanging open. I didn't know Grab had already moved so far beyond human. His dream of becoming an AI seems less absurd than it did a minute ago.

"That must be … pretty sharp."

Grab laughs. "Don't get all pouty, Twist. It's not like I'm cheating with your girlfriend or anything."

Kass's sad face flashes in my head, and a heavy fist squeezes my chest. Guess I don't have to worry about cheating anymore. I swallow down the lump in my throat and do my best to smile back.

"No, it's nothing like that. I'm just surprised, is all. I didn't realize how much you've upgraded yourself."

"It's happening, Twist." His face is dead serious. "I really am going to become an AI. Soon, I hope."

"Well, I guess if that's what you want … I hope it works out for you." I stammer, unsure what I'm supposed to say.

Part of me can't get past the fact that he plans to let his body die. I mean, even if his mind is copied into digital form, his original mind still dies, right? I sip my matte to cover my discomfort. I guess it's his body. If he wants to let it die, that's his choice.

I decide to change the subject. "Have you found out anything about Ianna?"

"Let me check." His irises become transparent, streams of data flickering within them. A frown creases the corners of his mouth, then the hazel returns and he focuses on me again. "Yes, sorry it took so long. The Carlyles' security system is tight. My seeker had to work hard to find a way in. I believe I've got her on security camera footage. But you're not going to like it."

My mouth goes dry, hope and dread warring within me. I take a deep breath and nod. "Show me."

A display window opens in the air, revealing a large room full of young children. There are dozens of them, ranging from infants to what I'd guess are four or five year olds. They're scattered around the room, playing with toys, chasing each other, laughing, crying. Doing childish things.

In one corner of the room a bunch of kids sit in a circle, assembling a large puzzle. An older girl wearing a white dress helps them, her eyes bright as she fits the shaped pieces into the developing picture. Her brown hair curls down her back, longer than I've ever seen it. Her face has filled out over the years. But I've seen that rapt, intelligent look in her eyes a million times.

Tears well up in my eyes as I watch Ianna methodically snap the puzzle pieces into place. In games of logic or memory, Ianna's always been uncanny. She'd wipe the floor with me every time. I want to leap through the screen and wrap my arms around her. I want to dance around the room. She's alive!

"She looks healthy. And happy."

"Keep watching," Grab says.

A sturdy woman with a slate-grey bun comes into the room. Mrs. Slate. Her face is dark, and she's brandishing a bamboo switch in her hand. All the children stop playing. Ianna's face crumples.

Mrs. Slate says something, gesturing angrily with the switch. Ianna flinches and nods. Mrs. Slate swings the switch viciously, leaving long welts across my sister's calves, below the hem line of her dress. Ianna curls into herself, but the blows do not stop. Mrs. Slate beats her bloody.

My fingers curl into fists, and I bite my cheek so hard I taste blood. I want to hurt this woman who hurt my sister.

The video ends, and the display winks out of existence.

"That's all I've got," Grab says apologetically.

"How recent is it?"

"Four days ago."

"Four days? That's when I was up there."

"According to the timestamp this is right after you were hauled away."

24

———————

"Spines, I was right there! She was so close!" I pound the arm of my chair with my fists. "I'm going back. I'm getting her out of there."

Grab nods. "I thought you'd say that. You're going to need help."

"No. If I get caught, that'll be the end of my Guardian career. Maybe the end of my life. I can't ask anyone else to risk that."

"You don't have to. I've already asked Shadow and Knott for you." He grins at me, obviously pleased with himself.

"I can't let them do that."

"Who says you have a choice?"

I turn to find Shadow standing there, Knott looming a step behind.

I shake my head.

"No. I really appreciate it, but I can't let you do that. You don't understand the risk."

"No, *you* don't understand, Twist." Shadow steps close, her dark eyes serious. "We're not letting you do this by yourself. You could get killed."

"It's better if I get all of us killed instead?"

"What did they teach us in the Games, Twist? Snatch and grab. Get in, get the objective, get out. This is what we've been trained for. We're a crew, we work together."

"But…" I look from Shadow to Knott to Grab. Gratitude, hope, fear, and guilt swirl through me in a bubbling stew.

I feel my future balanced on this moment. Ianna's future. Maybe the future of everyone.

I look into their eyes, each in turn. I find only resolve staring back at me.

Tears rise in my eyes again, but I blink them back furiously. I don't deserve this loyalty. I've been lying to everyone. They're my crew, my best friends in the world. They're willing to risk everything to help me.

Before they make this kind of decision, they deserve to know the truth.

I take a deep breath. My hands are shaking.

"OK, but there are some things I need to tell you first. Full disclosure. I'm not letting any of you go into this blind."

I think about swearing them to secrecy, but what would be the point? If they're with me, they'll keep my secrets. If they're not, no amount of swearing will keep them quiet. All I can do is pray I've judged them correctly.

So I tell them. I tell them about when I was captured by the Outsiders during our training. I tell them about my dad, and how the IEC has been lying to us all. I tell them I'm a secret double agent, waiting to be activated.

"But I can't wait any longer. Ianna can't wait. I have to get her out of there. Out of Canyon City. I'm going to take her to my dad, out to the scablands where she'll be safe."

I pause to catch my breath. Before I can continue, Shadow breaks in.

"I knew there was something you weren't telling me after that training exercise." But she's smiling as she says it. "I can't speak for anyone else, but I've been on the wrong side of the law my whole life. I might as well make it official and join the rebellion."

I gape at her. "Just like that? You know what they'll do to us if we get caught. You know we can never come back."

She shrugs. "What've I got to lose here? A bed in the barracks? A tin-plated job? Your friendship and your sister's life are more important than any of those things."

"What about your girlfriend?"

"Don't you know outlaws are sexy?" She narrows her eyes at me. "And I told you, she's not my girlfriend."

I don't know what to say to that, so I look at Knott instead.

The big woman nods decisively. "We are crew. Family. Family is the most important thing."

"But what about your family? If we join the Outsiders, you might not be able to see them anymore."

Knott's eyes are sad, but they do not waver. "My family is very big. They can take care of each other. But my crew is also my family. You are my family, and your family cannot take care of itself. I will help your family."

The tears are threatening again. I swallow the lump in my throat and turn to Grab. He returns my stare, head cocked to the side, his eyes serious for once. Long seconds pass, and I'm afraid I've miscalculated.

Out of all of us, he's the only one who grew up in Sunrise. His family has money and a big house somewhere. He didn't grow up in poverty and desperation. He has more to lose than the rest of us.

Finally, he chuckles and shakes his head. "You're dust-crazy, you know that? I mean, I already knew that, but you're really out there. Fight the IEC? Join the Outsiders? Do you even understand what you're saying? That's like saying you're going to stop Hera in her orbit. Without the IEC there is no Canyon City." He sweeps his hand around in an all-encompassing gesture. "Without the IEC none of this exists."

"Maybe," I say stubbornly. "Maybe not. All I know is, there's got to be a better way. You didn't grow up down in the dust where we did. Always hungry. Scrabbling to get by. That's no way to run a colony."

He shrugs. "Fair points, I suppose. It's largely moot, though. Until I figure out how to free my mind, I'm stuck here, tied down to a bunch of meat plugged into machines. I couldn't run away to the scablands if I wanted to."

"So you're out. That's fair."

"Slow down. I never said that. I'll help, I'm just going to have to be discreet about it. If I get caught, I can't bug out like the rest of you."

The tears finally break free, sliding down my cheeks in little rivers of joy.

"Thank you." I try to say more, but there are too many words, and there's something stuck in my throat.

Shadow wraps her arms around me, squeezing tightly. Knott joins her. After a moment, Grab does too.

Jmini clears his throat. "I've never been in a group hug before. Am I doing it correctly?"

I snort and Knott laughs, and soon we're all rolling around on the floor, cheeks wet with tears. Laughing until our stomachs ache.

25

Grab's realm becomes our war room. The couches and plush armchairs are replaced by a large, clean table, surrounded by conference chairs. We gather around it looking grim, cups of coffee and matte steaming before us.

Our host opens a map over the table. A topographical view of the Mesa hovers in the air, with Canyon City surrounding it on three sides. On the fourth side the wall can be seen, and the suggestion of scablands beyond.

He lights one area of the map. "The big assault on the scablands launches tomorrow. Which makes tomorrow night the perfect time for our rescue mission. Everyone will be focused on the attack. The guards should be lighter than usual."

"Until we get out into the scablands," I say. "Then we'll have troops to avoid."

"Have you ever seen a big battle, Twist?" Grab cocks his head at me. "It'll be chaos out there, and they won't be looking for people coming out of Canyon City. Plus, you'll be wearing Guardian gear. If anyone notices you, they'll think you're one of theirs."

"If you say so."

"I do say so. Now shut up and focus." He zooms the map in on

Sunrise. "The good news is they haven't increased security on the Carlyle estate. Not that I can see, anyway. I guess with you locked up, they figure the problem is contained."

"What are we going to do about that, anyway?" I ask. "Have you got a plan to get me out that won't set off every alarm in the mesa?"

"We'll get to that," Shadow says. "I'm working on it. Go ahead, Grab."

"As I was saying, the good news is the estate itself is not heavily guarded. The bad news is the estate doesn't need to be guarded because Sunrise itself is so secure." Red dots pop up around the perimeter of the map, indicating guard positions. "Getting so much as a wrist cannon into Sunrise would be difficult. Bringing any kind of force to the top of the mesa might be impossible."

I frown and lean forward in my chair, studying the red dots. "Can we get close-up shots of the guard posts? See what's there?"

"Sort of. I can hack into the security cameras at most of the posts, but how much they cover is questionable. There could be surprises sitting just outside the range of the cameras."

"You said there are cameras at most of the posts?" Shadow interjects. "Not all?"

"No, there are a few that don't bother with them." He gestures and three of the red dots on the far edge of the Canyon City side of the Mesa glow brighter than the rest. "These posts are so inaccessible that they don't bother. They don't expect anyone will try to climb up from Canyon City."

"So that's where we hit them?" Knott asks the obvious question.

"It's not that simple," Grab replies. "Those posts are lightly guarded because they're impossible to get to from that side. The cliffs in that area are beyond vertical, they're actually an overhang. So anyone trying to climb them would essentially be hanging backward over space. Also, they're crumbly and unstable, as you can tell from the big jumble of fallen rock at the base of the cliff."

"What about fliers?" I say. "Could a dart rig get up it?"

"Dart rigs aren't designed to go that high," Shadow answers. "If they could push off the cliff, we might be able to be use them as a kind of augmented climbing harness. But with that overhang, I don't think it's possible."

I take a sip of matte, swirling the warm liquid around my mouth as I think.

"I give up," I say. "What do we do?"

Grab and Shadow exchange a look. Grab gives the small girl a nod.

"Well," she says, "we could try to climb it the old-fashioned way."

"How's that?"

"With ropes and harnesses."

My eyes bug out of my skull. "I thought you just said that was impossible?"

"Difficult, not impossible. Don't forget, you're looking at the best climber in Canyon City."

"Well, that's great for you, but what about the rest of us?"

"That's what the ropes and harnesses are for. I'll be the lead climber and pick our route. You just have to follow. The augments in our armor will help us get firm handholds. As long as we set ourselves and support each other properly, the ropes will catch us if we slip."

"In case you've forgotten, I don't do well with heights." Even the thought makes me sticky with sweat, my heart thumping against my ribs. "Aren't there any other entry points?"

There are, and we spend hours discussing them. But they've all got drawbacks and challenges too serious to overcome. Inevitably, we end up back at the overhang cliffs, with everyone looking at me.

"You can do it, Twist," Shadow says. "I watched you climb a cliff in training. Just think of Ianna and don't look down."

I throw my hands in the air and bark a short laugh. "Sure, why not. Let's see how many impossible things we can accomplish in one day."

Knott smiles at me. "That's the spirit."

But that's just the first part of the mission. We still have to figure out how to break Ianna out of the Carlyle house and how to get away once we do. And how to break me out of jail without anyone noticing, before we even attempt any of the other steps.

Empty cups of matte pile up as we plan. Shadow masterminds the jailbreak, while I concentrate on the assault on the Carlyle estate. I sink into the realm of battlefield tactics, glad to be back on familiar ground.

When we finish, the faintest hint of sunrise lurks beyond the horizon, casting the canyon rim into dramatic silhouette. It's been a long night, and I'm exhausted and jittery from too much virtual matte.

"Well, it's a plan." Shadow twists her sleeve between her fingertips uncertainly.

Grab snorts. "It's a leap of faith into a dust storm, is what it is. Good thing we're not betting our lives on it. Oh wait, yes we are."

"It's the best we've got," I say, covering a huge yawn with my fist. "Last chance to back out. I won't think any less of you if you do."

Their tired, red eyes meet mine one by one. None of them look away.

"All right, then. Everyone get some sleep. I'll see you in" —my eyes flick to the blue numbers of the time display— "eighteen hours."

I close my eyes and rush back down the conduit to my cell. Hurtling toward the point of no return.

26

———————

Needing to sleep and being able to sleep are not the same thing. I toss and turn on my narrow bunk, my body exhausted but my brain racing. Every time I nod off, I jolt awake, startling myself from a dream of my friends going down in a rain of cannon fire, the smell of burning flesh acrid in my nostrils. Nightmare sweat greases my skin.

Thunder rumbles in the distance, repeated and insistent. Is the monsoon starting already?

Jmini sets me straight. "They're explosions, Twist. The attack on the Outsiders has begun."

Great. One more thing to worry about.

I give up and return to my pacing. I go over the plan in my mind, hunting for weak points. Unforeseen complications.

It's one big knot of unforeseen complications, as far as I can tell. This plan could go sideways in a hundred different ways before I even get out of my cell.

The explosions rumble on, a consistent reminder that even if we do pull off the plan, we're far from home free.

My heart races, my pulse pounding against my clenched jaw. It's hard to breathe.

I force myself to stop. Anxiety isn't going to help anything.

Back in Merrimac, Instructor Skinn taught us how to master our own bodies. To relax and focus. Stay in the moment.

I was never very good at it; my mind likes to race ahead. But if there was ever a time to get my thoughts under control, this is it.

I sit on my bunk and put my back to the wall. Close my eyes. Breathe in and out.

I try to focus on the air moving between my lips, over my tongue. Feel it filling my lungs. Hold it for two heartbeats. Release it slowly. Again.

Finding stillness is hard. Especially when my mind is churning at a million kilometers per hour, and the distant thunder keeps reminding me that people are dying out in the scablands. And one of them might be my dad.

Stop. Stop worrying about things you can't control. Focus on the things you can.

A lot of time passes, but I keep working at it, reining my mind in over and over.

My attention eventually settles on the warm spot beneath my collarbone. My greicagin shard pulses beneath my skin. It's a strange sensation, almost as if the crystal were alive.

Who knows, maybe it is. If the IEC scientists were willing to cover up the Horrors being sentient, what else might they have covered up?

My skin crawls at the thought of a living creature being implanted beneath my skin, even if it's as mindless as a reaper plant.

I know this is simple prejudice. Our bodies are full of other living creatures. Hundreds of species of bacteria and viruses live inside us in perfect harmony. We couldn't live without many of them. Symbiosis is an essential component of life.

Still, I don't like the thought. But I can't completely shake it either. The warm pulsing of the shard feels like blood pumping.

With an effort, I turn my mind away from it. My attention is caught by other things pulsing on a similar frequency. Things outside of me.

I extend my attention cautiously, reaching out, letting my mind travel on the shard's frequency. Yes, there are others. Other shards, other greicagins all around me, all pulsing in time with each other.

How have I never noticed this before?

I move my attention from shard to shard, breathless with astonishment. The shards are tiny, like mine, powering ventilation fans and strips of lights along the ceiling. There's even a sliver inside the door to my cell, energizing the locking mechanism.

I've become aware of a three-dimensional grid all around me, moving through the air in waves. I can see beyond the wall of my cell and intuit the shape of the space beyond it by the flow of energy through its systems.

There's a guard in the hall outside the cell block, and I map the system powering his augments. I turn my attention inward and realize I can trace the flow moving through my own augments as well. Delicate veins of force: a second limbic system inside me.

As I focus on my left arm, I feel the current increase to that area. I shift my focus to my right arm. After a few seconds, the warmth shifts in that direction as well.

I try to reverse the flow, pulling it away from the limb I'm looking at, back into the shard.

This is harder. The energy resists my efforts. It wants to flow out from the shard, not back in. My head begins to pound, but I stay with it, keeping my breath steady, focusing all my attention on pushing the flow up out of my arm. Slowly, it begins to trickle backward.

A crazy thought snaps my eyes open. Could I manipulate the power inside of other things? I look around for something to experiment on, and my eye falls on the tiny sliver inside the cell door lock.

That could be a dangerous game. If I fail, I might set off an alarm and jeopardize our careful plans.

I teeter on the edge of decision for long minutes, but in the end the temptation is too great. I have to know if I can do it.

I focus on the little box, and the tiny red greicagin sliver inside it. I trace the power flowing through the circuits. It seems simple enough. One circuit engages the lock, one disengages it. If I can coax the power to switch from one path to the other, the lock should open.

I close my eyes and still myself again, centering on my breath. Air whistles between my teeth, curling down, filling my lungs. I hold it. Release it slowly. Repeat.

When I feel completely in tune with the power, I return my focus to the lock. My headache comes back, stronger now, but I breathe through it, trying to concentrate. As I exhale, I push power along with my breath, willing it to shift from one circuit to another.

There's a soft beep. The door to my cell clicks open.

Electricity jolts through me. Equal parts elation and panic. Did I just trip a sensor somewhere? Are guards rushing in to question me? I'm frozen, waiting for an alarm to blare.

Nothing happens.

I cautiously allow myself to breathe again.

I get up and pad across the cell. I peer through the bars at the indicator light on the lock. It's green. Unlocked. I didn't just imagine that. It actually happened.

I fight against the urge to push the door open and run.

No. We have a plan. Shadow will be coming for me tonight. Stick to the plan.

I close my eyes and focus on the box, breathing power at it again. It's easier this time, now that I've learned the trick. The lock clicks shut, the indicator light shifting back to red.

I look around for another test and notice the security camera mounted on the wall. Like the lock, it has a tiny shard embedded in it. Like the lock, I deactivate it in an instant.

I'm shaking as I lower myself back onto my cot. Sharp spikes of pain stab my temples, in time with my heartbeat. I don't know what this is, but it's amazing. Everything runs on greicagins. Their power hums through the walls of every system in Canyon City.

My mind races with possibilities. If I can manipulate small systems like the lock box and security cameras, what else can I do? I look at the larger systems in the walls, the lights running through the ceiling. Can I affect them?

I'm itching to experiment further, but I need to be cautious. My head hurts so bad I can hardly see. I've pushed myself enough today. Besides, if I draw attention to myself, I'll tank the entire plan.

Tonight I have to get Ianna out.

Everything else can wait.

27

The lights go out at midnight. A second later, Jmini activates my night vision, turning the world green.

Here we go.

I close my eyes and find my breath, tuning in to the pulsing power of the shard within me. Once I'm focused, I move my attention to the security camera and the lock on my cell door. In moments, both have been disengaged.

Shadow comes through the door, dressed all in black, with a black scarf covering her mouth and nose. She starts when she sees me standing outside my cell, leaning against the bars.

"How did you get out?"

I shrug and grin. "I found a new talent."

She narrows her eyes at me. "If you could have gotten yourself out, you should have said so earlier and saved me the trouble of breaking in here."

"I just figured it out today. Besides, I know you put a lot of time into this plan. It'd be a shame to waste all that work."

"Whatever. Come on, Knott's waiting for us."

We slip out past the guard, who Shadow's got bound and gagged on the floor. I follow close but let her lead. She's the Covert, after all. If anyone can get us to the armory without being discovered, it's her.

"Remember the time we snuck down to Canyon City?" I whisper.

"That was jelly compared to this. Who knew our misspent youth would be such an essential part of our education?" I hear the smile in her voice.

We pad down the dark halls, stopping at every intersection to peer around corners before continuing. This level should be deserted after lights out, but you can never be too careful. It would be a shame if our entire plan was undone by an insomniac or a grunt sneaking in late from a night on the town.

Knott waits for us inside the armory, her stealth armor a flat black. She's standing over a pair of trussed-up guards.

"We were supposed to take care of them together," I hiss.

"You took too long getting here. I got bored. And when Lido here" —she nudges one of the trussed guards with the toe of her boot— "came wandering past where I was waiting in the hall, it was either take him out or let him raise the alarm. After that, there was only one guard left. I figured I should finish what I started."

"How very economical of you."

"I try. We have a long night ahead of us. Better if I eliminate a step, eh?"

"Can't argue with that logic." Shadow moves toward the racks of gear. "Let's go. Shift change isn't for hours yet, but if anyone discovers these guys before then, we'll have the whole base after us. We need to maximize our head start."

"Roger that." I move to the racks as well.

We get geared up in matte black stealth armor and full night assault rigs. Shadow's got a big black backpack and Knott has enough grenades and cannons for a small war.

I open a weapons locker and look with distaste at the spare warp-knives hanging there.

"Don't bother. I've got you covered," says Shadow.

She slips my warpknife from an inner pocket and tosses it to me. I snatch it out of the air, the hilt familiar and comforting in my hand.

The shard beneath my collarbone pulses, and I feel an answering pulse from the shard embedded in the hilt of my knife.

Is this pulsing a new thing? Or am I simply noticing it now that I'm attuned to the shards' energy? I put the question aside and clip the warpknife to my belt. Plenty of time to investigate later. Right now, we're on a tight schedule.

"Is everyone ready?" I ask.

Knott and Shadow nod.

"All right, let's do this."

We come out into an open loading bay, looking down over the lights of Canyon City. Bluish stars twinkle overhead and a steady breeze brushes the cliff face from the north. We're on level four, almost halfway up the enormous spire that contains the base and supports Sunrise atop its crest.

We argued about this part of the plan for a while. Shadow wanted to exit through the armory and make our way around the base of the Mesa on foot. I thought that route would take too long. Plus, if we went out the armory, we'd have to go down to ground level and climb back up from there. That may seem simple to Shadow but to me, skipping four levels of climbing is a huge consideration.

The downside of doing it this way is that we're not quite below the guard tower we're targeting. So we'll have to climb across the cliff horizontally while we're moving up it. Sub-optimal, but still worth it to save an extra four vertical stories, in my opinion.

Shadow takes the lead, clipping the rope to her belt and scampering across the face of the cliff like she was born there. I go next.

As soon as I move out onto the cliff, I realize our mistake. Saying the sandstone here is soft is a vast understatement. It crumbles beneath my grip like, well, sand without the stone part. Ten feet from the loading bay the cliff disintegrates between my fingers. For a heart-stopping moment I teeter backwards, and then I'm falling.

Fortunately, Knott hasn't left the loading bay yet. She shouts out, "Brace!"

Shadow goes rigid and together they arrest my fall. I dangle between them on the ropes, my breath rasping in and out. I make the mistake of looking down, and the night spins around me. Cold sweat covers my body in an instant.

After that, I use all the power I can muster from my armor to literally punch my hands into the cracks in the cliff face, often burying them up to the wrists. They still slip out half the time, forcing me to test each handhold before I dare to put any weight on it. It's a long, slow process, and it takes all my willpower to keep from hyperventilating.

Somehow, we make it to the overhang section. Clinging to the side of a cliff in the dark, eight stories up, I crane my neck back to find the cliff curving outward above me, forming a dark, sloped ceiling.

I think about how soft the rock is, and how heavy we are in our armor. I think about all the empty air behind me, and the jagged rocks at the base of the cliff. One wrong move and it'll be a long, slow fall to certain death.

28

———

"There's no way that'll support us."

My heart is hammering hard against my breastbone. I feel lightheaded. I think I might pass out.

"You both stay here," Shadow orders. "I'll go up and find an anchor point at the top. Then all you have to do is climb the rope."

I don't have a better idea, so I cling there like a pressure mine, praying some surveillance drone doesn't notice us.

Our armor is stuffed full of jammers and chameleonware that should make us virtually impossible to spot. Even watching her go, I lose track of Shadow thirty seconds after she leaves us. But still, you never know. If they've found the guards Knott tied up, they'll be out looking for us, and they'll know what kind of gear we're wearing. They'll be using every trick in the book to pick us out of the night.

As if he's reading my thoughts, Grab chimes in, "Don't worry, you're invisible up there. I know where you are, and I still keep losing you. There's no way someone searching blind could spot you."

"Did they find the guards we tied up yet?" I ask.

"I don't think so. I'm not reading any unusual activity on that level, and it'd be buzzing like a nest of red stingers if they had."

"Well that's one thing in our favor, anyway."

Minutes tick by like hours. My hands and feet are cramping, jammed inside the soft stone, and I have to carefully flex and relax them one by one. I'm getting worried about Shadow. It's been too long. She should be there by now.

"Grab, can you see Shadow?"

"I'm here, Twist," Shadow answers me. "I ran into some complications, but the rope is secure now. You can let go of the cliff and climb up."

"'Let go of the cliff.' You make is sound so easy. You have no idea what you're asking."

In order to grab the rope, I have to release my handholds. If I don't do it right, I could end up suspended from the rope again. Or worse, plummeting to a messy death eight stories below.

"One hand at a time," Jmini whispers in my ear. "Breathe. Take it step by step. You can do this."

I follow his advice and take a deep breath. Grit my teeth. I'm reaching for the rope in three. Two. One.

I pull my right hand out of the cliff and lunge for the rope. I reach too far, and it hits against my elbow. The movement pulls my other hand out of the sandstone and for a timeless second only my feet are attached to the cliff, my upper body slowly beginning to fall.

Then my hand finds a grip on the rope, and just as my feet slip free of the cliff, my second hand joins it.

I never thought I would miss clinging to that crumbling cliff face, but as soon as I transfer my weight to the rope, I wish I hadn't. I swing free of the rock, dangling out over space, suspended by a single dark strand. My weight makes the rope twirl, spinning me around so I'm looking out over the distant lights of Canyon City and the yawning blackness below.

"Spines!"

I squeeze the rope so hard I'm surprised I don't grind it to powder in my fists.

"Don't look down," Shadow advises.

"Too late." I pant and curse. "Dust, and spines, and red-bellied fire biters."

"One hand after the other." Jmini's voice is calm and sure. "You can do it. Your armor will lift you, you just have to tell it what to do."

I focus on the rope, narrowing my universe to the space right in front of me. Ignore everything else.

Somehow, I unlock one of my hands and thrust it up the rope, my fingers clamping desperately. I check my grip, then pull up with my biceps, my power armor smoothly assisting my effort. Then I thrust the other hand. Clutch and grab.

I laboriously repeat the process. Again. And again. And again. My entire world consists of clutching and grabbing, pulling up, and swaying in the wind on a dark strand of rope.

Finally, the rope rejoins the cliff face. I kick the toes of my boots into the sandstone, indescribably grateful to have footholds again.

I look up to find Shadow staring down from less than a meter away. Her hand is extended. I lunge upward and grasp it, letting her haul me up over the edge.

I roll onto my back and lie on the rocky ground, panting, staring up at the blue-white stars. I've never been so happy to be somewhere in my entire life.

When Knott joins us a few minutes later, I roll shakily to my feet. "All right. Where's the guard tower?"

"Already taken care of," Shadow says with a smile.

"What do you mean?"

"Do you see anywhere else I could secure a rope up here? I had to use the leg of the tower, and to do that I had to take out the guards."

"You've already secured the tower?"

"I just scaled the outside and slapped a disruption mine on the guard's armor. Jelly easy."

"You're amazing."

"I know. Now, let's get to the hard part."

We slip through the streets of Sunrise, silent shadows in the dark. Sunrise is a ghost town this time of night, unlike Canyon City, which would be crawling with thieves and hustlers. It's like we're on a different planet up here.

We crouch half a block from the Carlyle estate and go over the plan one last time.

"Once we get her, we've got to move fast," I hiss. "We'll only have a few minutes before the Guardians show up."

"Don't worry. We've got this." Knott's voice is calm and sure. Does anything ever ruffle her?

Thoughts for another time. Right now, we need to rescue Ianna.

My tongue flicks nervously over my lips. This is it. The culmination of years of searching. Everything rides on the next hour.

I meet Knott and Shadow's eyes. They seem calm and sure. Ready for anything.

"Thank you for being here. For being my crew. There's no one I'd rather have by my side right now." I swallow and blow out a short breath. The hilt of my warpknife is firm and reassuring. "Let's do this."

Ianna is waiting for me.

29

———

There's no way we can get in and out of the Carlyle estate without setting off a few alarms, so we're not even going to try. In fact, we're going to set off as many alarms as we can.

I sneak around to the back of the estate while Knott and Shadow get into position. If our information is correct, the servants are kept in a long, low building separate from the main house. I'm supposed to bust in there and grab Ianna while Knott and Shadow make a lot of noise at the front of the house. With any luck, I'll be gone before anyone even realizes I was here.

"I've got you all on my scopes," Grab says. "Everyone in position?"

A quick round of affirmative grunts.

"Ok, Shadow and Knott on my mark. Three. Two. One. Mark."

The night explodes with light and noise.

All the lights go on inside the house, and an alarm trills. Floodlights on the perimeter fence snap on, illuminating the gardens in stark white light.

The servants' quarters stay dark and silent. Just as I hoped.

I wait thirty seconds before I scale the wall enclosing the back of the estate, giving the estate's security forces time to focus on Shadow and Knott. Hopefully they'll believe they've pinpointed the problem and won't notice any new alarms that I set off as I scurry up through the back gardens.

I stop outside the dark servant's building, pressing my back against the stone wall beside the door. I've got some software that could disable the lock, but I think I've learned a better way. I close my eyes and focus on my breath, finding the thrum of the shard beneath my collar bone and the answering thrum inside the lock. I trace the power from the lock up into the wall, back to the building's central security system. I breathe a silent prayer for luck and deactivate it.

The lock clicks open. No new alarms sound.

A fierce grin splits my face as I slip into the darkened building. My augmented night vision makes the hall inside as clear as day.

This is where it gets tricky. There are several rooms Ianna could be in, and I've got no choice but to check them all. I'll need some help with this.

"Launch the drone, Jmini. You take the right side, I'll take the left."

"Aye aye, Capitan."

I move quickly down the hall, stepping as silently as possible. At the first door I press my back to the wall and reach down to test the handle. Unlocked. Good.

I count to three and pivot, throwing the door wide while leveling my cannon at a room full of bunk beds. There are six on each side, sleeping twenty-four people per room. A wide aisle runs down the center. Someone is standing in the aisle, and they jump and squeak as I fling the door open.

"Ianna," I hiss. "Ianna are you in here?"

Blanket-wrapped shapes sit up in their bunks, but no one speaks.

"Does anyone know where Ianna is?" I ask, louder this time.

The person standing in the aisle clears their throat. A male voice says, "The girls are down the hall."

I move on to the next door, and the one after that. Each time, the scene is repeated. Each time, they send me further down the hall.

Sweat runs down my temples. This is taking too long. The Guardians will be here any minute.

As I open the next door, a dark shape comes flying at me. I swing my cannon toward it, but they're on me before I can fire. Something hits me on the side of the helmet, the crack of wood meeting metal incredibly loud in my ears. My training takes over and I grab and twist, hurling my assailant through the air. Instructor Skinn would have been proud.

The figure slams into the wall behind me, and a high voice cries out in pain. I'm back on my feet in an instant, cannon trained on the room, ready to meet other threats. Nothing comes at me. The rest of the servants huddle in the narrow slots between bunks, hiding behind the bed frames.

"Ianna," I bark. "I'm looking for Ianna. Is she here?"

Nobody responds, so I grab the nearest cowering shadow and shove my cannon into the woman's face. I don't have time to ask nicely.

"Ianna," I repeat.

She points a shaky finger at the crumpled figure that attacked me.

"Ianna?" I move toward the figure carefully, wary of another trap. She grunts and moves away from me.

"Don't come any closer spine-sucker."

The voice is older, but the tones are still familiar. I lower my cannon and drop to my knees, raising my visor.

"Ianna, it's me. It's Theo."

"Theo?"

"Yes," I croak, my throat tight with emotion.

She moves forward hesitantly, peering into the darkness of my helmet. An interior light pops on above my forehead.

"There. That'll help," Jmini says.

Ianna's eyes widen. "Theo. It really is you."

I nod and pull her into my embrace. She yelps and pushes away as my arms close around her, and I drop her like a hot ember. She collapses to the floor and curls in on herself, whimpering.

"Ianna?" I'm squatting over her, hovering uncertainly. I reach a hand toward her face, but she flinches away.

"Don't touch me," she snaps.

"I'm sorry, did I hurt you?"

She draws a shaking breath, hissing the air between her teeth, fighting to control herself.

"It's not you, it's me. Just don't touch me, ok?"

"Of course." I hold my hands up in surrender.

Jmini clears his throat.

"I hate to be a party pooper, but Grab informs me that the Guardians are on their way. You might want to save the reunion for later."

"Ianna, we have to go. Right now. The Guardians are coming, and we don't want to be here when they arrive."

"The Guardians?" Her nose crinkles in confusion. "What are you, Theo?"

"I'll tell you later. Put your shoes on. There's no time right now."

"OK."

"Package located." I whisper into my comm, while she scampers off to grab her shoes. "Status?"

"It's a real dust storm out here, Twist," Shadow responds. The sound of cannon fire is loud in her feed. "We're pinned down by estate security."

"Be ready to bug out in sixty seconds," Grab tells her. "I've got Guardians incoming."

"Roger that."

"Ianna," I hiss. "It's time to go."

30

I anna gasps as we step out under the star-filled sky and wraps her arms around herself. It's cold, and she's only wearing a thin night-gown and shoes.

"We'll get you somewhere warm soon. For now, running will have to do the trick."

She nods and we're off, sprinting across the gardens toward the back wall. She yelps and falls as we're navigating a row of grape vines. I curse my stupidity. Of course, she doesn't have night vision. She can't see a dust-licking thing out here.

"Are you all right?" I kneel beside her, reaching out my hand to help her up.

"Fine." She flinches away and scrambles back to her feet. "Let's go."

We're almost to the garden wall when Grab chirps, "Time's up boys and girls. Get out of there now!"

"Bugging out," Shadow confirms.

A large explosion lights the night on the other side of the compound. Probably Knott's idea of a diversion.

We reach the wall, grey stone blocks stacked three meters high. Clinging ivy covers the surface.

"Give me your foot, I'll boost you over," I say.

Ianna shoots me a contemptuous look and scrambles up the facade as easily as a plakbeetle. She straddles the top and looks down at me.

"You coming?"

"Show off." I grin, then use the power in my armor to vault up beside her in a single leap.

She arches an eyebrow. "I'm the show-off?"

We scramble down and dash into the darkness. We're heading for the northwest corner of Sunrise, where the mesa butts right up against the scablands. Shadow and Knott are still making loud noises on the other side of the Carlyle estate. The sounds of fighting grow distant as we approach a lighted guard tower.

I motion Ianna down behind a stand of lanbrush.

"Stay out of sight. I'll be right back."

I approach the tower from the backside, away from the lights and explosions. When I reach the circle of light surrounding it, I break into a sprint.

My luck holds. The guards are staring out the other side of the tower, mesmerized by the lights and explosions. I've scaled the tower and slapped a pair of disruption mines on their armor, cutting off their power before they even know I'm there. Their armor goes dead, and they fall to the floor of the tower.

Ianna trots over, my heart swelling as she emerges from the darkness. I can't believe I've finally found her. I realize I'm grinning like a fool.

"Grab, bring in our taxi."

"Already on its way."

We dash across the hundred meters of empty space beyond the tower and stop at the edge of the mesa. The cliff cuts away before us, a wide expanse of empty air falling to the scablands far below. My knees wobble at the height, and I take an involuntary step back. Cold air burns my throat, rasping in and out in thick plumes. Hera's light pinks the horizon, but luckily neither moon has risen yet, which means that for at least another few minutes we're no more than a pair of shadows in the inky night.

At least it's quiet out there; the assault seems to have paused. That's one lucky break, anyway.

I turn to Ianna. "We have to jump."

"Jump? Are you insane?"

"Believe me, I don't like it either, but it's the only way off this mesa. Don't worry. My gravboots will float us down as gently as a feather."

Ianna looks skeptical. "Where are we going, Theo? Isn't that the scablands out there?"

"Yes. We're going to the scablands."

Her eyes go wide. "You really are insane."

"Look, I'll explain everything when we get there. I need you to trust me. We don't have much time."

Cannon fire streaks across the sky, underscoring my point.

Ianna flinches and glares at me. "Fine. But only because the alternative is going back to that estate. Your plan sucks spines, Theo."

"It'll make sense when we get there, I promise."

I reach for her, intending to lift her up. She ducks away from my arms. I grunt in exasperation.

"You have to let me carry you down."

"Not like that, I don't. Turn around."

I do as she says and her arms close around my neck. Her body presses against the back of my armor.

"Are you sure? It'll be safer if I hold you."

"I'm sure," she growls. "Let's go."

My feet and hands tingle as I look into the void, trying not to think about how far it is to the ground. The last time I did something like this was in training. Back then I froze, and Knott had to throw me over her shoulder and carry me down like a sack of flour.

Now I'm going to jump. Of my own free will. With my sister on my back.

My knees tremble. My breath puffs in frightened little clouds.

"You can do this, Twist." Jmini's voice is soothing. "Your gravboots have got you. Don't think, just jump. On the count of three. One. Two."

I step off the edge.

Ianna squeaks, and her arms squeeze my neck so tight it's hard to breathe. Of course, I'd have trouble breathing even if I was alone.

Balancing on my gravboots is tricky with a passenger. I have to lean forward to compensate for the weight on my back, which makes me feel like I'm going to tip onto my face. This doesn't help my anxiety.

The dark wall of the cliff rises beside us, an endless black expanse scrolling upward. Our descent is so gentle, I'd hardly even be able to tell we were falling without it.

"It's just like Alice in Wonderland," Jmini says. "Down, down, down, she fell."

"What are you blowing about?" I croak.

"Alice in Wonderland. A delightful old allegory. The protagonist, a young girl named Alice, falls down a deep hole. She floats down rather like we are now, gently falling and falling and…"

"Jmini! You're not helping!"

My boots crunch down onto gravel. I sway and stumble forward before catching my balance. Ianna releases my neck immediately.

"Aren't I? I think I managed to distract you quite nicely. You're welcome."

I sigh. There's nothing worse than a smug AI.

My gravbike glides out of the dark and settles onto the ground beside us.

"Package received, Grab."

"Roger that. Now get out of there fast, Shadow and Knott have an entire squad on their tail. I've got to go too, I can't risk one of my drones getting shot down and traced back to me. You're on your own."

"Thanks, Grab. Take care of yourself."

"You too. Now get going!"

I pop an emergency blanket out of the saddle pack, and Ianna wraps it around her torso. I marvel at this new, much larger version of my sister as I carefully seal the edges of the foil-like material together.

"Not perfect, but it'll help with the chill. It's going to get real cold when we start moving."

I settle myself on the gravbike and gesture for Ianna to climb on behind me. She hesitantly slides her leg over the saddle.

"Wrap your arms around my waist and hold on tight. I'm going to get us out of here as fast as I can. Whatever you do, don't let go."

She grips my armor, holding her rigid body as far away from my back as she can.

The gravbike hums softly as we rise off the ground. I steer us around the perimeter of the Mesa, my sister's weight behind me making my heart sing. I set a course for the scablands, and the rising sliver of Hera. We accelerate into the light like the dawn of a new day.

31

───────

Ianna tightens her grip as we plunge down a long, gradual incline toward the scablands. I can't say I blame her. It looks like we're plunging to our death, racing down the massive slope hundreds of meters to the ground below. I wish I could reassure her, but she doesn't have earcones with comms built into them under her helmet. Or a helmet, for that matter. She's just going to have to trust me on this one.

This plunge is metaphorical as well as physical. The edge of the Sunrise mesa acts as part of Canyon City's wall here, so by jumping off it, we've leapt out of the city. Down into the scablands we go.

Cannon fire flickers in the darkness to my left.

"Knott, Shadow, what's your status?"

The line is silent for a long moment, and I fear the worst. Then Shadow's voice comes.

"Don't worry about us. You deliver that package."

I hear cannons in the background, and long streaks of color flicker across the night over our heads.

I grind my teeth against conflicting urges. My crew is in danger over there because they chose to help me. Every cell of my being screams to go help them.

"I'd advise against that." Jmini reads me like a map. "They are supposed to be a distraction, and I must say they're doing a fine job of it. I'm quite distracted. If you go over there, you defeat the whole purpose of the exercise. You will make their efforts meaningless."

"I know, Jmini. I don't need a lecture."

But I did need it, and I'm secretly glad he gave me one. Each of us has a role to play in this mission. Mine is to get Ianna to safety. I've got to trust Shadow and Knott to take care of their end as well.

It still doesn't help the sick feeling in my stomach every time the cannons flicker.

Focus on the task at hand, Twist. Control what you can control.

We hit the end of the slope and level off abruptly. Ianna tenses against my back. If she makes any sound, it's lost in the wind. I hope she's not too cold back there. My display says it's near freezing in the bottom of the canyon. The blanket I wrapped around her is an excellent insulator, but there are parts of her body it doesn't cover well. Her hands and feet, for instance.

I lean forward and throttle up. The faster I get her to safety, the faster I can get her warm.

The soft light of Hera streaks the sky, but it hasn't touched the canyon floor yet. Down here it's black as the bottom of a mine. My night vision won't be enough at this speed.

"Jmini, digitize."

The night disappears, replaced by a three-dimensional line rendering of the landscape. The topography extends away from me in lines of green and yellow. For some reason this calms me. It's like being back in the Game. Even though I know it's an illusion, I feel safe here. In control.

Five minutes later I pull the gravbike into the rendezvous point and set down. I can't believe we escaped so easily. My gut says it was too easy. I look to the sky, searching for the telltale glint of a drone tracking us. I don't see anything. Without Grab around, it's impossible to know for certain.

I hustle Ianna inside the cave. She stumbles over the rocks, unsteady on her frozen feet.

"Now what?" she asks between chattering teeth.

"Now we get you warm and wait for my friends."

I sit her down and check her hands and feet. She won't let me touch them, so I have to content myself with a visual examination. They're white with cold, but I don't see any obvious frostbite. I won't be able to tell for certain until they warm up, though. I make her rub them together, then tuck the blanket around them and cross my fingers. It's all I can do for now.

I peer out of the entrance to the cave. Nothing but darkness outside. No response on my comm either, which isn't much of a surprise. There's too much rock in the way for a signal to travel very far down here. Shadow and Knott are on their own.

I pace back and forth, from the entrance to Ianna and back again. She watches me warily.

"Are you really a Guardian, Theo?"

"Not anymore." I mean it as a joke, but it doesn't sound funny. I've just thrown away all our security and safety. What comes next is anyone's guess. "And I go by Twist these days."

"How did that happen?"

"Which part?"

"Becoming a Guardian. I didn't know rockheads could do that."

"Normally they can't." Talking distracts me from my worry, so I keep going, telling her all about qualifying for the Guardian Tournament, and my struggle to get through it. When I get to the part about Dad, she stops me.

"Dad's alive?" Her voice veers between hope and disbelief.

"Yes, he is."

Ianna stares into the dark of the cave, her face puzzled.

"I don't know what I'm supposed to be feeling right now. I'm happy Dad's alive. And I'm glad we've escaped. But I'm terrified we're outside the wall. And I'm terrified the Carlyles are going to come after me. It's too much to process."

"That's fair." I squat down in front of her. "The important thing is we're together. We can be a family again."

"Yeah." Her voice is skeptical.

"What is it?"

"I spent years in that estate. They did horrible things to us. A lot of people died. Where were you? Why didn't you come for me sooner?"

I'm cut by the accusation in her voice.

"I was a deep diver in one of the mines. I looked for you, but I couldn't find you. I did what I could."

"I guess it wasn't enough," she says bitterly.

"Are you saying I could have done something more? I was as trapped as you were. I looked for you for years! I'm sorry it took so long, but I've got you out now. Doesn't that count for anything?"

She looks at the floor.

"I'm sorry too. It does count. It counts for a lot. But you're my big brother. You were supposed to protect me. I kept waiting and waiting for you to come. The first year or so, every time something bad happened, I'd think, 'Everything will be OK when Theo gets here.' But you never came, and time passed, and I stopped waiting. And part of me started blaming you for letting me down. For letting all of those terrible things happen to me."

"What terrible things? Is that why you don't want to be touched?"

"I don't want to talk about it. I'm out now. Let's focus on that." She looks up and meets my eye. "I'm grateful you got me out of there. Thank you. But I've been angry with you for a long time. It's going to take a while for my feelings to shift."

My stomach feels hollow, like I've been punched. What happened to my sister? What did she go through that left her so damaged?

I want to push her, demand details. Instead, I lock my jaw shut, clamping down on my impatience. There will be time for that later.

I nod and say, "I understand."

But I don't understand. I don't understand at all.

32

———

There's a sound in the darkness at the back of the tunnel. I whirl, cannon in one hand, warpknife in the other. My night vision shows me three figures slipping out of a narrow passage, their armor ragged and mismatched. Outsiders.

As they get closer, I recognize my Dad leading the group. He shines a red light at my face.

"Hi, Dad. I brought you someone." I nod toward Ianna.

The light illuminates her, and then there are tears, whispered words of joy, and an attempt at a hug that Ianna avoids.

My dad looks tired, but his eyes are shining. "Let's get you two to safety."

"Take Ianna inside. I'm going to wait here for my friends."

I step to the front of the cave and peer out into the rosy night. All is quiet and still.

Dad hesitates, then nods and presses a small dataspike into my hand.

"Here's a map of the cave system. I trust you'll destroy it if it comes to that. Be safe. I'll see you soon."

Then they're gone, melting back into the darkness.

I listen until the crunch of their footsteps has been swallowed by silence, then I return to the front of the cave. The moonlight makes a pink line across the dust.

I'm too restless to sit still, so I pace back and forth, staying inside the darkness, peering out at the light. Every minute feels like an hour. Where are Shadow and Knott? What if they don't make it? Have I gotten my friends killed?

Guilt and fear gnaw at my guts. This is why I never told them I was working with the Outsiders. This is what I always knew would happen.

My heart almost stops when a voice comes out of the darkness behind me.

"Fancy meeting you here, boy."

I whirl to find the ragged man from the wall watching me. His eyes shine with a metallic sheen.

"What are you doing here?"

He snorts. "I live out here. The better question is what are you doing here?"

"I brought my sister."

He nods as if that explains everything. "Family ties bind the strongest of all."

"Are you an Outsider?"

"Not exactly."

"Not exactly?"

"Our goals often coincide. I have certain talents that are useful to them. We have an understanding." He cocks his head, considering. "I understand you have certain talents as well."

"I don't know what you mean."

"You helped my friend with the wounded leg."

"You mean that Rock Horror in the cavern? What happened there? Could it understand me? What do you know about that?"

"I know many things about that Horror. Yes, she could understand you. She's an old friend."

My mind reels. I sit down abruptly.

"Who are you?"

"No one of consequence. Once I was called Steel. Now I'm merely an old blade."

"Steel? Like Captain Steel from the stories? What was he, your grandfather or something?"

His lips curve into the hint of a smile. "Something like that."

I take in his ragged robe, his bent back and gnarled fingers.

"Well you sure don't look like Steel now. Rust maybe."

"As you say." He inclines his head in acknowledgement. "Rust suits me. A blade long past usefulness."

"What did you mean when you said 'she' told you? Who is she?"

"Her name isn't translatable."

"Do you really expect me to believe that you talk to Horrors?"

He shrugs. "Believe what you wish. Or don't. It's all the same to me."

I stare at him, my suspicions about the IEC and the Horrors turning over in my mind.

"Are they really intelligent?"

"What do you think?"

"I think I shouldn't draw too many conclusions just because I survived one encounter with your friend."

"Skepticism is wise. You should always find your own truth."

"What about…"

"Shhh." He shushes me with a raised palm, his eyes shining as he stares past me into the darkness. "Someone's coming."

I draw my warpknife and whirl, crouching in a defensive posture.

"You're as twitchy as a Horror, Twist." Shadow steps out into the moonlight. Her faceplate glows softly atop her scorched armor.

"Didn't anyone ever tell you it's a bad idea to sneak up on Horrors?" I growl. "That's a good way to get your head snapped off."

She tries to smile, but her eyes are tight, and there's no joy in them. "Hazards of the trade."

"Shadow, this is…" My voice trails off. The ragged man, Rust, is gone.

Shadow cocks an eyebrow at me. I wave her off.

"Never mind. Is Knott with you?"

Shadow shakes her head. Ice pierces my chest.

"She never showed at the rendezvous point."

"Spines!" I pound the boulder with my fist. "I never should have asked her to help."

"It was our choice, Twist. We knew the risks."

"We'll never get anywhere if we lose someone every time we rescue someone else."

"As far as I know, Grab is OK. So we've still got an inside man."

"Assuming he hasn't been clocked too."

She shrugs, her lips pressed into a thin, hard line. "He knew what he was signing up for. None of us went into this blind or unwilling, Twist. Give us that much credit."

I take a big breath and blow it out. "I know, I know. You're right. That doesn't make it any easier."

She places a gloved hand on my shoulder.

"That's what makes you a good commander. You care about your soldiers. But this is war. Bad things are going to happen. Things you have no control over. Just remember that every one of us made our own choice to be here. Carrying all of the guilt on your shoulders disrespects that choice."

I look into her eyes, wise beyond their years.

"Thanks, Shadow. That doesn't make it any easier, but it's nice that you said it. Can we go get Knott back now?"

"I am here."

Knott stumbles into the cave. Her armor is in even worse shape than Shadow's. Some of the parts have been melted to slag, and her entire left arm is exposed.

"Knott!" I throw my arms around the big tank. "I thought we lost you. I've never been so happy to see someone in my life!"

She laughs. "I am happy to see you too."

I ignore the wet trails on my cheeks.

"Come with me, I want to introduce you to my family."

33

My family has seen better days.

Dad looks like he's been stretched thin. He's grown a patchy beard, and dark hollows lurk beneath his protruding cheekbones. The fungal scabs on his bald head have multiplied, forming an odd-looking crown of browns and greens.

Ianna is twitchy and withdrawn, sitting with her feet pulled up onto her chair, knees folded against her chest, arms wrapped protectively around them. We've wrapped her frozen feet in two pairs of thick socks, and her pale hands clutch a steaming mug of tea. Hopefully she doesn't have frostbite. From the looks of this place, I doubt they've got the medical facilities to treat it if she does.

Not exactly the family reunion I envisioned.

We're sitting around a camp table, perched on folding chairs. A small light illuminates our faces from below, creating dark shadows and unnatural planes. The rough cavern feels unsafe, and me and my crew still have our armor on, though we've removed our helmets.

This cave complex isn't nearly as polished as the last one I was in. The tunnels are rough and natural, carved by wind and water instead of human hands. More like the unmapped systems I used to deep dive in than anything I'd expect to see inhabited.

We've ended up in a huge open cavern, along with what looks like half the Outsider population. There are gear bags piled everywhere, with twitchy-looking Outsiders curled in sleeping bags beside them. The main assault may have just started yesterday, but from the dark hollows beneath these people's eyes, I'd guess the Guardians have been hounding them for weeks.

I wonder if I've made a terrible mistake. Maybe Ianna was better off in Sunrise. Maybe we were all better off. Maybe I've just sentenced us all to death.

"Are you warm enough?" Dad hovers uncertainly over Ianna.

She curls in tighter around her tea. "I'm fine."

His hands pet the air uncertainly. He obviously wants to comfort her in some way but has no idea how to do it.

"Can I get you anything? Some soup, or…?"

"I said, I'm fine." Ianna snaps. "You're dead, remember? Dead people can't help the living."

Guilt drags Dad's head down. He stares at the floor.

"I'm sorry about that. I didn't have a choice. Me being dead was the only way to keep you safe."

"Safe? Keep us safe?" Ianna's voice rises, her eyes widening. "You call abandoning us to the streets of Canyon City keeping us safe?"

"The Guardians found out I was working with the Outsiders. They would have locked me up and taken you away. They wouldn't have only punished me for my work. They would have punished you too."

"Maybe you should have thought of that before you decided to become a terrorist. Maybe you should have thought of your family first."

Dad's jaw tightens.

"I was thinking about my family. I was thinking about your future in this colony. Do you want to be indentured slaves your whole lives? Working off a debt you can never repay? Do you want to pass that on to your children? And your children's children? Does that make you feel happy? Is that the life you want?"

Ianna squirms in her chair, but she doesn't back down. "No, the life I wanted had my dad in it, and my brother. The life I wanted had my family all together."

"So did mine!" Dad shouts. "All together and free of the IEC and their Guardian lapdogs!"

They stare at each other, eyes smoldering. I can almost see the heat rising off them in waves. They look so alike in their anger, it's scary. The way they pinch their foreheads, the set of their jaw.

I can remember a hundred similar moments growing up. Ianna and Dad were built the same way, and they've always butted heads because of it.

Watching them go at it brings a lump up in my throat. It's good to have the family together again.

Dad looks away first.

"I'm sorry, Ianna. I truly am. I did the best I could for our family. For all the families." He waves his fingers out over the cavern.

I follow his gaze, taking in the families in their dirty sleeping bags. A woman sits nearby, playing with her daughter, some kind of elaborate hand-signal game. The woman's dirty blonde hair hangs over her shoulders in lank, unwashed clumps. The girl is about five years old and filthy, her clothes more holes than anything. Still she's smiling and laughing, completely losing herself in the game in the unselfconscious way only children have.

It makes me sad to see them looking like homeless refugees. I remember how clean and neat their base was when they captured me during training. The floors were wide and level. Lights everywhere.

Now the only light comes from free-standing collapsible lamps, and much of the cavern is in darkness. The Guardian offensive has hit them hard.

Dad reads the concern on my face.

"This is one of a number of temporary hiding holes. We need to stay mobile now. Since the governor was killed, the Guardian attacks come without warning.

"It's not as bad as it looks. There are a lot of groups like this out there. We stay decentralized, so if they get one group, the others can continue the fight. We switch locations every couple of days so the Guardians can't zero in on us."

"So the war is going well?" Shadow leans forward in her chair.

Dad's mouth turns down.

"That might be stretching it. They've been keeping us scrambling. It's hard to stay organized when you're constantly on the move. We're on the defensive right now, but give us a couple of weeks and we'll get this thing turned around."

I can't tell if he believes what he's saying or if he's trying to make himself believe it for our sake. Either way, he's putting up a brave front, and my heart constricts with painful memories at the look in his eyes. He used to wear the same look when he had to deliver hard news when we were kids.

"You've been running all this time?" I ask.

He nods wearily.

"It's been exhausting. Staying one step ahead of the Guardian strikes has taken everything we've got."

I look around at the ragged people curled in their sleeping bags. Clearly, they can't keep this up forever. There's got to be a better way.

I wonder how many Outsiders there are out here in the scablands. I've seen hundreds in this complex myself, and I'm sure I haven't even seen all of it. There could be thousands.

Multiply that by who knows how many groups…

Maybe I'm emboldened by the success of our raid on the Carlyle estate. Maybe I'm just reckless.

Either way, I lean forward.

"Why run? Why not strike back?"

Dad's brow crinkles. "Fight back? We just want to be left alone. Live our lives in peace and quiet and freedom. Besides, do these people look like they can fight back? We're exhausted from running. We've barely got enough food to stay alive."

"Which is exactly my point. You can't keep running forever. Why not fight back now, while you still have the strength to make a stand?"

Shadow nods thoughtfully. "The best defense is a good offense."

"If the Guardians are busy defending Canyon City, they can't keep chasing us all over the scablands," I add.

"Maybe." Dad doesn't look convinced. "Tactics aren't really my strong point. I'll set up a call with Tempest in the morning and you can discuss it with her. For now, we should all try to get some sleep while we can. The shelling in the canyons makes it impossible to sleep during the day."

As if his words have summoned it, exhaustion rolls over me, so heavy I can barely keep my eyes open. The thin pad on the ground I'm given feels like the softest bed. I sink beneath the surface of sleep without a trace.

34

Explosions rip me from sleep. I'm crouching on my feet before I've even got my eyes open, warpknife clutched in my hand.

"Someone's raring to go." Ianna's sitting at the camp table, a steaming cup of tea pressed between her palms. Her mouth curls in a tight scowl.

Her eyes never stop moving, flicking around the cavern like a bird in a cage. She's wearing a brown pair of pants and an old grey sweater three sizes too big for her that someone gave her last night. The skin on her hands looks a little splotchy.

"How are your hands? Do they hurt or feel numb?" I ask.

She shakes her head, not looking at me. "No, they're fine."

I study her for a minute, trying to figure out if she's lying. But what reason would she have for that? They're her hands. If she says they're fine, I guess they're fine. That's one bullet dodged, anyway.

All around us people are rolling out of their sleeping bags, cooking breakfast, brushing their teeth, doing their morning routines. Another distant explosion sounds. Pale dust drifts down from the ceiling. Nobody looks alarmed, or even in much of a hurry.

"Are we under attack?"

"No, this is the way we start every day." Dad points at a table by the wall. "Breakfast is over there. Go grab a plate."

My face burns as I sheath my warpknife, feeling foolish. The smell of the food makes my stomach rumble.

I find Knott standing behind the table at the breakfast line, serving plakbeetle meal cooked with spinach. I raise an eyebrow at her as she places a large spoonful on a plate and hands it to me.

"What are you doing?"

"Helping," she says simply. "In my home it is the same. Cooking, serving, and eating takes many hands. Food makes family."

The round-faced man standing beside her smiles and adds a scoop of fried mushrooms to my plate.

"Your friend is a wise woman. She knows her way around a kitchen too. We'll be lucky to have her around here."

Knott beams at the compliment. I don't think I've ever seen her look so content. I know her family works in the greenhouses, but I never thought about how that might shape her relationship to food. It looks like she's going to fit right in here.

Another explosion shakes the cavern as I grab a cup of matte and join the others at the table. More dust falls, sprinkling the surface of my matte with white flecks.

"You start every day like this?"

Dad shrugs. "I call it our twenty-one gun wake up call."

Shadow snorts, then chokes as tea goes up her nose. She coughs, her eyes watering. I pound her on the back.

Dad sets a plate of mushrooms on the table in front of Ianna. She doesn't acknowledge him, but after a moment she picks up a small mushroom and puts it in her mouth. I smile to myself. Peace offering accepted.

Across from Ianna sits a short, thick woman with dozens of scrap metal hoops piercing the outer edge of her ears. Her face is wide and flat, her dark hair cropped short. A finger-long scar runs across her left cheek. She feels kind of like a miniature version of Knott, if Knott were half a meter shorter and a decade older. Dad sets a hand on her shoulder, and she reaches up to squeeze it.

"Ianna, Theo. I'd like to introduce you to Mai."

I raise an eyebrow at Dad, then smile and nod at Mai. "Nice to meet you."

Ianna, predictably, says nothing.

"Congratulations on getting out of Canyon City," Mai says. Her voice has a faint accent I can't place. "It's not an easy thing to do. I know your father is glad to have you here."

"I just wish it was under better circumstances," Dad says.

"What's your role in all of this?" I ask, gesturing vaguely at the cavern around us.

"I work in security," Mai says. "It's my job to keep everyone safe."

"So you're a fighter." Shadow says. It's not a question.

Mai inclines her head. "When I have to be."

"Someday we won't have to fight anymore," Dad says over her shoulder.

Mai pats his hand fondly. "We all have our little dreams."

"You don't believe in peace?" I ask.

"Oh, I believe in peace. But I don't believe we're going to get there by running and hiding. The only language the IEC understands is power and violence. We can't keep running away and expect them to leave us alone. We have to show them we can fight back. Make them respect our strength. Only then will we have peace."

"I respectfully disagree," Dad says. "Peace can't be achieved through war. You have to live the life you want in order for it to become reality. If we prove to the IEC we're no threat, they'll leave us alone eventually."

Mai smiles up at him fondly.

"You father is an idealist. It's one of the things I like about him. But unfortunately the world doesn't work the way we'd like it to."

"You think we should fight back? Attack Canyon City?"

Mai nods. "Yes, I heard about your suggestion. I think it's a good one. I look forward to discussing it with Tempest. But these things can wait until after breakfast. Eat. Your food is getting cold." She follows her own advice, and digs in.

Halfway through breakfast an alarm blares. Around the cavern, people start frantically gathering their things.

Dad curses quietly. "Now we're under attack. Grab your gear and prepare to evacuate."

The explosions get louder and dust falls thick as snow. The ground trembles. People start heading for a tunnel at the back of the cavern. They move quickly, but their retreat is orderly and calm. They've clearly done this before.

An explosion rocks the cavern hard, knocking people off their feet. My matte tips, spilling across the table, dumping hot liquid into my lap. I jump up, cursing.

"Time to go. Hurry." Dad's got a deep furrow between his eyebrows, and he keeps glancing at the entrance.

I slept in most of my armor, so it only takes a minute to slap on the final pieces. Shadow does the same. Knott's across the cavern, helping the kitchen crew pack.

I'm wondering if I should go get her when the cavern starts to shake in earnest, the ground bucking so hard I can hardly stand. Chunks fall off the cavern wall, huge rocks cracking, falling and rolling. People scream and start to run.

The tip of a huge metal drill breaches the wall, scattering Horror-sized rocks as if they were sand. The drill rolls forward, more visible every second, chewing its way into the cavern.

"Tunnel diver," Shadow gasps beside me.

I can only nod in mute astonishment. Seeing Castle's projection of a tunnel diver was one thing. Seeing the real thing in action, watching a two-story drill chew through a solid stone wall like it was mist, is quite another. Especially when it's coming right toward you.

"The Guardians have arrived." I turn and frantically push Ianna into motion. "Run!"

35

The Outsiders' orderly retreat dissolves into screaming chaos. People are pushing and shoving, scrambling to get away from the deep diver and the Guardians who are surely right behind it. There's too many of them, and the tunnel they're running for is too narrow. They'll never make it in time.

"Shadow! We've got to set up a defense. Hold them back long enough for the civilians to escape."

Shadow nods, her eyes bright and calculating.

"We need Knott," I say.

"I am here." The big tank appears beside me, stepping of the chaos as if conjured by her name.

I nod up at her.

"Perfect. As soon as that drill stops spinning, Guardians are going to come flooding into this cavern. We need to keep that from happening as long as we can."

"Well, they've only got one entry point," Shadow says. "That bottleneck works in our favor."

"Yes," I agree "Let's set up a defensive triangle, with the entry point as the tip. Hopefully we can fool them into thinking there are more than just three of us."

"There are more than just three of us." Mai steps up beside me, clutching a small cannon. Half a dozen hard-faced Outsiders stand with her.

They're wearing patchwork gear, and their armor and weapons look like they're at least twenty years old. I doubt they'll stand up to more than a blast or two, but I suppose that's still better than nothing.

I give Mai a grateful nod.

"Excellent. Let's spread out and concentrate our fire on the entry point. With any luck, we can keep them contained long enough for the civilians to escape."

Mai gets right to work, deploying her people quickly and efficiently.

I turn to find my dad hovering uncertainly on my other side. He has no armor, but clutches a well-used cannon like he knows which end is which.

"I want to help," he says.

"Get Ianna to safety." I point him toward the escape tunnel. "She's all alone and she doesn't know anyone here. I didn't bring her all the way out here just to lose her at the first sign of trouble."

"But…"

"Go! We've got this. Please, Dad."

I think it's the *please* that gets him. He frowns, but nods reluctantly.

"All right. Be careful, Theo."

"You too, Dad. I'll see you soon."

The rumble of the giant drill changes pitch. The massive cone slows and stops spinning, then starts to back out of the hole. I brace the cannon against my shoulder and aim at the widening gap it leaves behind.

The first Guardian appears, silver armor framed perfectly in the gap. Then everyone fires at once, and the figure is blown backward.

This makes the Guardians cautious, and they hunker down and return fire. For a few minutes the world is nothing but cannon fire: red and yellow pulses flashing across the cavern.

This is exactly what I hoped would happen. The longer we keep the Guardians focused on us, the more time the civilians have to evacuate. I keep glancing over my shoulder, checking the progress of the stream of Outsiders flowing away. It's going more slowly than I'd like, but they're making progress. Another couple of minutes, I think.

Then the Guardians charge, and our time is abruptly up.

Silver armored figures come pouring through the gap. Ten, twenty, thirty of them. Our cannons take out a few, but the rest just keep on coming. In moments, we'll be overwhelmed.

"Retreat! Run!" I shout.

This is no time for a last stand. We held them for a few minutes. That's all we hoped for.

"Get to the escape tunnel," Mai says. "There are charges set inside the entrance."

"Roger that."

I pound across the cavern, cannon fire lighting my way. The Guardians are coming after us, but they're moving forward at a cautious pace, keeping their lines together. Our headlong flight should get us to the tunnel before them.

The last handful of civilians slip into the tunnel ahead. I allow myself a grim smile of satisfaction. Our delaying action worked.

Then one of Mai's people tumbles to the ground beside me. I pivot and start to pull the man up, then I realize he's got no legs. The Guardian's cannons have cut him in half.

I drop the lifeless torso in horror.

I turn and almost stumble over the mother and daughter I saw playing earlier. Now they lie lifeless on the ground. They're still holding hands. Beside them sprawl a blood-soaked pair of teenage boys.

Civilians who didn't get out fast enough. Innocent people caught in the crossfire.

We may have saved some of them, but we obviously didn't save everyone. My satisfaction slides into sadness, and quickly flares into anger.

These people didn't do anything to deserve this. They were only trying to live their lives in peace. The Guardians broke into their homes and killed them. And they'll keep doing it unless we stop them.

I'm the last of our team to pass through into the mouth of the tunnel. Mai is standing a hundred meters down, counting heads. She nods as I pass, then thumbs a trigger clutched in her fist.

The world explodes behind me as the charges go off. The tunnel collapses, thick dust filling the air. I pull my scarf up over my mouth and nose and shoulder my cannon as I turn to face the settling debris. My finger is tense on the trigger as I wait for a glint of silver armor. For long moments all I see is dust swirling.

Then Mai calls out. "It's sealed. We're clear."

I sag against the wall, suddenly exhausted as the adrenaline drains out of me. Mai catches my eye and nods beneath her scarf. I nod back, but it's a tired, unsatisfied nod.

We accomplished our goal. We held back the Guardians long enough for the civilians to escape. But it wasn't enough. People still died.

We can't keep doing this. The Guardians will hunt us wherever we run. The tunnel divers will let them dig us out of every hiding place. We're only delaying the inevitable.

We have to fight back.

36

While most of the Outsiders head off to their next hiding place, Dad leads us to a small entrance cavern. We sag against the walls, stunned and horrified. Weak light filters in the opening, illuminating the clouds our breath makes in the chill morning air.

I cup my hands, blowing on my fingertips.

"It's cold out here. Monsoon season's going to start any day now."

"That's one of the nice things about living underground," Dad says. He tries to smile, but his mouth gets stuck halfway, and ends up in a grimace. "The temperature stays pretty consistent no matter what it's doing on the surface. It's warmer in the winter and cooler in the summer, just the way you want it."

He sets up a communications rig on a tripod and we all sit within range of the camera. Mai and her hard-faced Outsiders join us. Their gear is scorched and dented, but well-cared for.

Tempest's head flickers into view on top of the rig. Her dark skin is ashen beneath her silver dreadlocks, and bruised circles lurk beneath her eyes. She looks like she's aged ten years in the past few months.

"Alton, report," she says simply.

"The base has been compromised. The Guardians dug us out with one of those new drills they've got. We were able to slow them down and get most of the people out. I'd estimate a dozen casualties. The survivors are on their way to area E-twenty." Dad says this in a flat voice, as if he's reading a report. Like if he doesn't keep the words at a distance, he won't be able to say them. Tempest curses but motions him to continue. "I've also got some new recruits for you. This is Shadow and Knott and my daughter, Ianna. I'm sure you remember my son, Theo."

Tempest's eyes narrow. "Twist? What are you doing out here? You're supposed to be our inside man."

I slide my eyes sideways and shuffle my feet.

"I'm sorry. Ma'am. Circumstances dictated that I had to get out."

"What circumstances were those?"

"I needed to rescue my sister. I'm sorry if I messed up your plans, but my family comes first."

"You're a soldier, Twist. You should know how to follow orders better than that." She scowls, her eyes hard. "Who have you brought with you?"

"This is Shadow and Knott. Knott's the toughest tank in Canyon City and Shadow's an excellent covert operative. In fact, I'm sure she knows more about the interior of the Mesa than I do."

Tempest looks at them suspiciously.

"Why are you here? Why would you leave your cushy life to come hide in a cave with a bunch of rebels?"

Shadow meets her gaze calmly. "Twist is my crew. If he needs me out here, this is where I'm going to be."

Knott simply folds her arms, nodding in agreement.

Tempest weighs them with her eyes for a long moment before turning to Ianna. "This is your daughter?"

"Yes."

"You should have stayed put, girl. Out here dodging bombs is no place to be."

"Anything is better than where I was." Ianna's voice scrapes like rusty metal.

Tempest raises an eyebrow at her tone, then shrugs. "It's your life. Keep your head down and run fast, and you might even get to keep it for a week or two."

My dad's brow creases. "Are things that bad, Tempest?"

"We're losing ground every day, Alton. Pulling back further and further. One of these days we're going to run out of places to hide. When that happens, we'll have no choice but to stand and fight."

"Would that be such a bad thing?" I ask. "Isn't fighting the whole reason you're out here?"

Tempest looks at me with scorn. "You've just come from the city, kid. You know what kinds of armor and weapons the Guardians have. Have you seen anything out here that can stand up to that stuff? No. Because we don't have it. The day we stand and fight is the day we die."

"Then why did you provoke this response?" Shadow interjects. "Why kill the governor?"

Tempest stares at Shadow like she's grown a second head.

"You think we killed the governor? Why in the world would we do that?"

"Because you're Outsiders? Because that's what you do?" Shadow's face screws up in confusion. "I don't know, you're the General. You tell me."

"We did not kill the governor," Tempest spits the words. "Killing the governor would be stirring a sand stinger's nest with a stick. That would be one of the stupidest things we could do."

"If you didn't kill the governor, who did?" I ask.

"Who killed your mother?" Dad says quietly.

"Oh, come on, Dad. The Guardians didn't kill the governor. I was there. Guardians were killed in that attack."

Tempest shrugs.

"Maybe not all of the Guardians were involved. It could have been a splinter faction. Who gained the most from the governor's death?"

My mind immediately goes to the funeral duels, to the governor's box and the IEC representatives.

"Julius."

Shadow's eyes widen as the pieces click into place. "That little spine-sucker. Why didn't he get caught?"

"There are two explanations that I can see," Tempest says. "One, because everyone believed that we did it, so they never looked for a second culprit. Or two…"

"He had help," I finish. "Someone high enough in the Guardians command structure that they could steer the investigation away from him."

"Castle." Shadow looks disgusted.

I nod. "Castle. I bet he's been working with Julius the whole time."

"While it's nice to know who our enemy is, I don't see how that helps us in the short term," Tempest says. "No matter what the justification is, we're still getting stomped out here."

"Which is why we need to attack," I say.

"Attack? Are you out of your mind? They've got superior numbers and superior weapons. It's all we can do to stay one step ahead of the bombs out here. How are we going to attack?"

"Twist is right. It's what they'll least expect," Shadow says. "We could catch them with their pants down."

I start to pace, my thoughts churning.

"They've just launched their big offensive. Most of their forces are outside the wall. If we can get behind them, the command structure will be vulnerable. If we're lucky, we might even get through to Julius himself."

Shadow's eyes light up. "The observation deck."

"The observation deck," I agree.

"What's this observation deck?" Mai leans forward, her eyes sparking with interest. She looks from me to Shadow and back.

"It's a platform up on the side of Merrimac where Guardian command stands during major actions. From there, they've got a clear view of the scablands for several kilometers," I explain.

Mai's forehead creases. "Wouldn't they be able to follow the action better through drone cameras?"

Shadow chuckles. "Yes, they would. It's some throwback alpha-male guano. Standing up high and directing the troops."

"And you think this platform will be vulnerable?"

"Most of the troops will be outside the wall. If we can sneak inside their perimeter, we can catch them by surprise."

Tempest's eyes tighten as she weighs this information. Finally, she nods.

"OK. I'll give you command of a small team. If you can take down their leaders, you could change the complexion of the entire war." She turns to my dad. "Alton. Take Mai and whoever else you want. But keep it small. Quality over quantity."

Dad nods, his face somber.

"Kill Julius." Ianna's voice is raw, her fists balled so tight I can see her nails digging into her flesh.

I stare at my little sister. What did they do to her on that estate?

This is my fault. I should have found her sooner. I should have never let them take her away from me in the first place.

I look her in the eye.

"I'll get him, Ianna. He'll pay for what he did to you."

37

———

The morning of the raid dawns grey and damp. Clouds stack up on the edge of the canyon, releasing a steady drizzle that promises to become harder as the day progresses. The monsoon has finally arrived.

I only get all of this through Jmini's drone feed. We're underneath the Mesa by the time the sun crests the horizon, in the dust and dark where the smuggler's tunnel meets the sewer. We've been moving since well before dawn. There are seven of us in the team. Me, my dad, Shadow and Knott, plus Mai and two of her soldiers, Lonc and Des.

The Outsiders look like another species in their mismatched, piecemeal armor. It reminds me of Wayfinders, and the old patched-together gear I used to qualify for the Guardian Tournament. That gear was trash compared to the training shell I was assigned in Merrimac. I hope their armor is more effective than that.

"Charming." The hoops in Mai's ear jingle as we step over a stream of sewage.

"I always said I'd take you to the best places." My dad shares a smile with her, and I wonder at their relationship.

Shadow catches me looking and smirks. "Yeah, I think they are too."

My cheeks grow warm. I don't think I'm ready to discuss my dad's sex life.

I wonder if we're throwing our lives away. Our plan is audacious enough to succeed, but it could also turn out to be suicidal. I wonder if my desire for revenge is making me reckless. I catch my dad looking at me. I didn't want him to put himself in danger with us, but he refused to stay behind. After three years of believing he was dead, it's weird to look up and see him in his mismatched armor and boots, staring at me. I keep wanting to pinch myself to see if I'll wake up.

"It's strange, isn't it?" he says softly.

"You don't look the way I remember."

He chuckles. "Imagine how I feel. You were just a little kid when I ran. Now you're taller than I am, and thicker in the shoulders. I have to fight to keep from doing a double take every time I look at you."

He shifts his weight from foot to foot.

"I'm sorry I got you into this, Theo. I thought I was keeping you safe by running away. Taking the struggle with me and keeping you out of it. Instead we're crouched in a dark tunnel together, on our way to assassinate someone." He sighs. "Probably not the best parenting."

"You didn't get me into anything. I chose to be here. If anyone's to blame, it's me. I was supposed to keep Ianna safe and I didn't. That's the reason we're here now. I should have never let them take my little sister away."

"You can't blame yourself for that. You were just a kid."

"You don't know, you weren't there. I could have resisted. If I'd kicked up enough of a fuss, they might have kept us together. But I didn't. I stayed silent and let them take my sister."

"But you got her back."

"I got someone back," I correct him. "Someone that only vaguely resembles the sister I remember."

"Everyone changes. It's part of growing up. That version of Ianna would be gone even if you had stayed together. You can't blame yourself for biology."

"Biology?" The word is sour in my mouth. "Is that what they're calling being abused by Sunrisers these days? Biology?"

"You don't know she was abused."

"Yeah, I do. I can see it in her eyes. Ianna's broken. And the only way to fix her is to break Julius."

"You know violence only begets violence, right?"

"That's ironic, coming from the man who abandoned his children to join the revolution."

He looks sheepish. "I guess we all learn at our own speed."

We fall silent. He's right, of course. Violence does beget violence. But we didn't start it, they did. The IEC forced my grandparents to come here. Kept all of us as indentured workers for generations. They're reaping what they've sown.

My dad clears his throat.

"I want you to know that I'm proud of you, son. Proud of the man you've grown up to be. I see you in that armor, frowning the same way your mother used to … I just wanted you to know that, whatever happens, I'm proud of you."

"Thanks, Dad." I look at my feet, embarrassed. But a fierce joy kindles in my belly. Embers that have been banked for years struck into sudden flame by his words. Warmth flows out through my limbs, and it's all I can do to keep the grin off my face.

"We'll be a family again," he continues. "I promise. When this is over, we'll be a family like we were always meant to be."

I swallow around the lump in my throat. I nod, not trusting my voice.

He nods back. No more words are necessary.

Jmini chimes softly in my ear. I go rigid, and everything comes into sharp focus.

"Today's attack is starting," I hiss.

The crew grips their weapons. We're like duelists poised at the start of a bout. Coiled and tense. Ready to explode into violence.

The ground trembles. Crimson dust drifts down, speckling my armor. The sound of distant explosions tells me it's begun.

Shadow has gone ahead to scout, so the rest of us are stuck waiting. Sitting here imagining the worst.

I project Jmini's drone feed for everyone. A column of silver Guardians flows into the scablands like liquid mercury. They ride in tanks and transports and heavy walkers. There are thousands of them.

My breath catches. They are going all out with this assault. They really intend to wipe the Outsiders from the scablands.

My dad's face is pale. Mai fidgets with the straps on her armor. Knott's lips are pressed in a grim line.

I tighten my grip on my cannon. Even if the plan works perfectly, Julius won't be unguarded. Under the best-case scenario, we're still going to have to fight.

We watch the column split into branches, thin lines of troops flowing down side canyons. The enormous tunnel divers rumble along behind them. I can't believe how big the machines are. They look like buildings with teeth.

The Guardians shoot bombs into every cave they come to. I count the rumbling explosions. One. Two. Three. Four. A cliff face collapses, an avalanche of rock and dust blots out an entire canyon in a blink. The vibrations travel up through the soles of my feet, cause the palms of my hands to itch.

Time drags. Still no word from Shadow. The waiting is driving me crazy.

"Jmini, can you see her?"

"Negative, Capitan. Sending a drone up there wouldn't be the best idea."

I'm gripping the cannon so hard my fingers start to cramp. More bombs explode. Another cliff collapses. And another. If we don't do something soon, the scablands will be nothing but rubble.

"Let's go." I slap my visor down. "We can't afford to wait any longer."

"What about Shadow?" Knott asks.

"We'll catch up with her on the way."

I start to move, not waiting to see if anyone is following. I'm relieved when I hear the clanking of armor that tells me they are.

We climb out of the tunnels and into the Mesa itself, the dusty underground giving way to clean, polished stone. It's strange skulking down the familiar halls. This was my home a few days ago. Now it's an enemy encampment.

Energy running through the walls tickles my awareness, like an itch between my shoulder blades. The halls are arteries, with greicaginfueled blood running through their veins. Every light fixture burns like a miniature star.

I'm viewing the world with new eyes. I don't know how I never saw it before.

The Mesa seems deserted, just the way we'd hoped. Everyone is out taking part in the attack.

Still, doubt gnaws at me as we approach the platform.

"Where is Shadow?" Knott whispers, echoing my thoughts.

"I don't know. Be ready for anything."

I motion everyone close. They cluster around me, faces grim, excitement and fear flashing in their eyes.

"This is it. The platform is around the next corner, a hundred meters away. We need to go in fast. Stay low and keep your cannons ready. This is our chance to chop off the head of the snake. We're only going to get one crack at it, so let's make it count. Any questions?"

"I have a question." Julius steps into the hall, with six Guardians flanking him. My stomach drops as I recognize Rory and the towering bulk of Ghengis.

"Did you really think you could waltz in here like you own the place?"

38

"I could ask you the same thing," I snarl.

Julius's smile doesn't touch his grey eyes.

"Unlike you, I do own the place." He turns to Ghengis. "I want him alive. You can kill the rest."

We dive for cover as the Guardians open fire.

My crew is pinned down along the walls of the tunnel, cowering in doorways. Our ambush has been sprung, but not the way we intended. Julius knew we were coming.

Lonc screams, his cannon dropping. His breastplate curls away from an ugly black hole blown through its center.

I extend my periscope, but a cannon blast sears it off before I can get an accurate read on our assailants.

"Spines! How many are there, Jmini?"

"It's impossible to say. Judging from the frequency of the cannon blasts, I can say with 98.2% accuracy that there are more than seven and less than twenty."

"Great. Thanks for nothing, Jmini." I chew my lip, thinking furiously. A steady stream of cannon fire keeps us pinned down.

Across from me, Des leans out and fires two quick shots into the darkness. Before she can pivot back behind cover, a cannon blast burns her head to ash. The headless corpse stands for a moment, looking confused, before collapsing to the ground. Against the Guardians' advanced weapons, the Outsiders' armor is practically useless.

"We're getting slaughtered, Jmini. Any ideas?"

"Run?"

"You know, I'm starting to have my doubts about the 'intelligence' part of Artificial Intelligence."

"You're free to come up with your own ideas."

"Looks like I'll have to, doesn't it?"

I lean out and fire off a few shots. Incoming cannon fire ricochets off my armor in red streaks, blowing holes in the walls and filling the corridor with dust.

"OK, I've got an idea. Dad, do you read me?"

"Theo? Are you all right?"

"I'm fine. Listen, Dad, we're getting killed up here. We've got to fall back."

"Tell me something I don't know."

"I've got a way to get us out of here, but you've got to trust me."

"Something tells me I'm not going to like this. What've you got?"

He's right, and he doesn't like it, but he goes along with it anyway.

"On my signal, Dad and Mai run. Knott, you're escorting them. Three, two, one. Now!"

I dart out of my doorway, cannon blazing as fast as it can cycle. Knott steps out as well, her heavy armor shedding cannon fire like water.

Return fire punches my breastplate as I sprint across the tunnel. My armor turns the blasts away, but they still hurt. For the handful of seconds it takes me to cross the tunnel, it feels like I'm being pummeled by Ghengis.

I dive into another doorway and press my back to the wall. My breath rasps inside my helmet. My armor glows faintly, warmed by the cannon fire.

"Dad, are you there?"

Silence is the only response. Icy panic stops my heart. I can't lose my dad again.

Then the com crackles to life.

"We made it," he gasps. "Are you OK?"

"I'm fine. No damage. Let's do it again. Knott, on my mark. Three, two, one. Now!"

I dash back across the tunnel, drawing enemy fire again while Knott retreats with my dad and Mai behind her. We repeat the maneuver four more times.

Sweat trickles down my forehead, burning my left eye. My armor is red hot, pulsing with heat. The inside of my helmet reeks of over-heated carbon. It's still turning away the cannon fire, but I don't know how much more it will bear.

"Jmini, what's my armor status?"

"You're pushing the upper limits of the tolerance range. If you keep this up, there's an eighty-six percent chance of system failure."

"Spines. Dad, can you read me?"

"Faintly." His voice is soft, which is a good sign. It means he's managed to retreat far enough down the tunnel that the rock is inter-fering with the com.

"How far are you? Are you out of sight lines?"

"Almost. There's a bend just ahead. Maybe two more dashes should get us around it. How are you holding up?"

"Fine."

The truth is I'm feeling like a roasted shellbaby in my overheating armor. Two more dashes and I'll be one big bruise from head to toe. If my armor doesn't give out entirely.

I'm not going to tell him that, though. The armor the Outsiders are wearing is so poor it's hardly worth the trouble. The Guardians' cannons will slice through them like warm jelly. Their only chance is for me to keep drawing fire until they're clear.

"All right," I say. "On my mark."

The tunnel lights up as I hurl myself into space once again. I don't try to aim my cannon; I just point it up the tunnel and depress the firing stud. I've got my head down, counting the steps between me and the opposite wall. Time stretches, each foot moving with agonizing slowness. My armor is white hot, the air inside my helmet sweltering. It's so bright I can't even see where I'm going. A cannon blast punches me in the ribs, spinning me around. I slam into the wall and fall onto the stone. I roll over, struggling to get back on my feet.

"Lie still, Twist," Jmini says. "It's OK. You're out of the line of fire."

"Oh good." I groan and collapse onto my back.

The heat radiating off my visor makes my face feel sunburned. I shove it open, letting the cool tunnel air flood in. My armor is so bright it lights up the entire tunnel around me.

"I guess there's no hiding from them now."

"No," Jmini agrees. "There's a ninety-nine percent probability they know right where you are."

"Good. All eyes on me. That was the plan."

"It may be working a bit too well. I don't know if your armor can survive another pass. Even if it does, how do you intend to sneak away when you're glowing like a comet?"

"One thing at a time, Jmini. I'll cross that bridge when I come to it. Right now, I've got to let my dad get away. That's all that matters." I roll over and point my antenna down the corridor. "Dad? What's your status?"

"Almost there. One more dash should do it. How are you holding up? Your armor is shining like a star. Are you sure it can handle that much punishment?"

"I'm fine, Dad. You just get to safety. I'll be right behind you."

"OK, we're ready whenever you are." Doubt creeps into his voice, but he doesn't question me. Which is good. I don't have the energy to spare on an argument right now.

"All right, give me a minute."

I push myself up to my feet and suck a last gulp of cool air before closing my visor. One more. I just have to get across the corridor one more time. Ten steps. Jelly easy.

"On my mark. Go!"

Halfway to the other wall, I realize I'm not going to make it. Cannon fire hits my left leg above the knee, and instead of deflecting off my armor, it punches straight through, searing my thigh like a branding iron. The force of the shot yanks the leg out from under me and slams me face-first into the ground.

I'm exposed and immobile.
I'm dead.

39

The incoming fire pauses, the Guardians waiting to see if I'll move, waiting to see if they got me. My leg burns. I don't know if it will bear my weight.

I look to the right, careful to move only my eyes, measuring the distance to the corridor I'm angling for. Three meters. Jelly easy. I tuck my arms into my chest and start to roll.

The cannon fire starts up immediately, lighting up my head and shoulders. It's so hot inside my helmet I can hardly breathe. But I don't need to breathe. I just need to keep rolling.

Finally, I get behind the wall. I shove my visor open and gasp in the cool air, grinning like a madman. Safe. My dad is safe. I've done my job.

My dad's voice in my earcones is anything but calm.

"Theo are you all right? Theo, answer me!"

"I'm fine, Dad." I try to say it casually, but the pain in my voice gives me away.

"What's wrong? Are you hurt?"

"Just a flesh wound, Dad. Nothing to worry about." I look down at my leg as I speak, hoping my words are true.

The armor over my thigh is blackened and twisted around a fist-sized hole. The flesh within the hole looks like overcooked plaksteak, the charred surface streaked with bloody red threads. Jmini has hit me with some pretty good localized painkillers, so I don't feel much, but it looks pretty bad.

"Spines."

"What is it?" My dad sounds frantic.

"Nothing. I'm fine, Dad. Keep going. You and Mai get to safety. I'll catch up with you soon."

"You don't sound fine. You sound hurt."

"Yes, I am hurt. But not bad. Don't worry. Just go!"

"I'm not leaving you, Theo."

"Dad, you leaving me was the whole point of the plan! I'm the distraction, remember? I'm the one with Guardian armor. If you don't leave me, then what did I do all of that for?"

"You did it for the same reason I'm not leaving without you. We're family. I told you I'd never leave you behind again, and I meant it. Now, can you walk? Or do I need to come get you?"

"Dust, Dad. This is ridiculous."

But his words have kindled a warm glow in my belly. We're family. My dad is not going to leave me behind again.

"Jmini, any ideas?"

"We could get you a metal leg like Grab has."

"I'm serious. The Guardians watched me go down. They'll be coming to see if they got me. We don't have much time."

"I could launch a drone to see where they are."

"That's a waste of a drone. They'll burn it down before we get any useful intel."

"It seems to me you could use a distraction of your own."

"What am I, ground plakbeetle?" Shadow's voice breaks in over the com.

"Shadow? Where are you?"

"I'm behind your little playmates."

"You usually are. If you draw their attention, will you be able to get out after?"

"Are you kidding? I could sneak out of Guardian headquarters during a lockdown."

"Isn't that exactly what's happening now?"

"Huh. So it is." I can hear the smile in her voice. "I happen to have a couple of spare bombs. Will that work?"

"That'll do. And if you happen to blow up Julius and Ghengis, I won't complain."

I grit my teeth and use the wall to lever myself up to my feet. My leg twinges when I put weight on it, but not as bad as I feared.

"Those are some good painkillers, Jmini."

"Remember they only kill the pain, they do not repair the damage. Try not to exacerbate your wound too much by running on it."

"Only as much as I have to." I take a deep breath. "OK, Shadow. Any time you want to make a big boom."

"One big boom coming up. May the sun be at your back, Twist."

"Yours too. See you on the other side."

The walls shake, and an enormous plume of dust shoots down the center of the tunnel.

I'm moving before the tremors die, limping off into the depths as fast as my wounded leg will carry me. Not the smoothest retreat, but I'm more concerned with results than appearances.

For ten meters I'm alone with the dust, and I dare to hope that I've gotten away. Maybe Shadow's distraction worked. Spines, maybe it did better than that. Maybe it took out the whole strike force.

Then cannon fire rakes across the back of my armor, putting an end to my fantasy. I'm knocked forward onto my bad leg, and it buckles beneath me. I cry out, extending my hands to break my fall.

Someone catches them.

"No falling down on the job." Dad slings my arm over his shoulder. "Come on, we have to keep moving."

Cannon fire chases us. There's not as much as there was before Shadow's distraction, but there's still enough to worry me. I try to angle my body so my armor is shielding my dad, but with him half-supporting me it's almost impossible.

I hold my breath and count the distance as we lurch forward. Ten meters. Twenty.

Dad grunts and jerks forward, then sags against me. Now we are supporting each other.

"Are you all right?"

"Fine." His face is ashen, teeth bared in a grimace. He's as bad at lying as I am.

The warmth in my belly ices over. We're not going to make it.

Cannon fire erupts from the dust in front of us, lancing past our shoulders, back toward the Guardians. Knott and Mai are laying down cover fire.

They're firing blind through the dust of Shadow's blast. But that's OK, because the Guardians are firing blind too. With any luck, the return fire will make them pause. Give us enough time to slip away.

I hitch Dad's arm over my shoulder and lurch forward into the darkness. I'm bearing his weight. He's bearing mine.

40

———

"Where are you hit?"

Dad grunts. "Don't worry about it. I'm fine."

We struggle forward, the tunnel barely visible in the red glow of our stealth lights.

"You are not fine. Where are you hit?"

"Left side," he concedes. "But I'm fine. I don't think I'm bleeding."

"That's because the cannon that hit you cauterized the wound. It doesn't mean you're fine."

The scent of his charred flesh makes me sick. Odd how it smells so much worse than my own wound did.

We've left the smooth halls of the Mesa behind, and are now moving through a narrow crevice, single file. Mai has the point. Knott hangs back, playing rearguard. We haven't seen any cannon fire in over a minute, and I hope we've seen the last of it.

My leg burns. I want to get a look at Dad's wound, so when the crevice widens into a small cave, I call a halt.

Dad wheezes as I lower him onto a flat-topped stone. "We need to keep going. They'll be right behind us."

"We will. But first I need to check on your wound."

He grumbles but lifts his arm so I can see. It's a lot deeper than he let on. One of his ribs gleams at the bottom of a long, seared trough of cooked flesh.

"Well, you were right. At least it's not bleeding." I pull disinfectant spray from my med-kit. "This is probably going to sting."

He winces as I spray the wound, but to his credit he doesn't cry out, even though the disinfectant probably burns as much as the original wound. He always was a tough duster. I remember him picking me up and telling me to walk it off when I fractured my arm as a kid. I flex my fingers with the memory, sadness washing over me.

My dad's forehead creases as he sees my expression. "What's wrong?"

"Just thinking about home."

"Now is not the best time for nostalgia. Those Guardians could be here any time."

"I can do two things at once, you know." I tuck the disinfectant away and spray liquid bandage over his wound.

"You don't have to get snippy."

"I know what I'm doing. I took care of myself just fine after you abandoned us."

Dad's eyes widen, then his face gets red.

"And your sister? You did a great job of taking care of her. That girl's so messed up she won't go inside during a dust storm."

"That's my fault? You left us!"

Knott's voice hisses from the dark. "They are coming!"

I jump to my feet, embarrassed I let myself get so distracted. I guess it's true what they say: No one gets under your skin like family. I can feel the Guardians coming as soon as I turn my attention to the crevice. Half a dozen greicagin shards moving our way.

"They're about a hundred meters out. We've got to get moving."

I help my dad up, and he leans against me stiffly, though I don't know if the stiffness is anger or his wound. Frankly, I don't care. He left us without parental guidance. He has no right to blame me for the way we turned out.

We hobble on, not speaking to each other. I'd forgotten this side of him. The dad who gets mad and doesn't talk to you for the rest of the day. Funny how details like that get glossed over in your memory.

I try to ignore my dad and focus on the Guardians tracking us. I count the shards, trying to figure out how many there are. There are more shards than soldiers though, and it's hard to count them individually when they're so close together.

"Jmini, can you see how many Guardians are back there?"

"That's a negative, Capitan. The rock interferes with my scans. Would you like me to launch a drone?"

I chew on that for a moment.

"No, don't bother. We'd better save them."

"Aye aye, Capitan." Jmini sounds obscenely cheerful.

"What are you so happy about?"

"Well, this is all rather exciting, don't you think? An armed pursuit through darkened caverns. It's terribly romantic.

'Half a league, half a league,
Half a league onward,
All in the valley of Death
Rode the six hundred.
'Forward the Light Brigade!
Charge for the Guns!.'"

"Six hundred?" I snort. "There's something wrong with your math."

"It's poetic license, Twist. Tennyson's metaphor is not constrained by truth."

"Neither are you, apparently."

"Poetry!" he exclaims. "Sound the charge!"

I chuckle and shake my head. Crazy AI.

I glance at my dad, still grinning. "Do we know where we're going?"

"Of course we do. We use this route into the city a lot." He scowls, glancing behind us. "I don't like that we're leading the Guardians down it, though. We're going to lead them right to our camp and burn one of our secret entrances in the process."

"Maybe we should stop leading them then. Maybe it's our turn to set an ambush."

Dad peers at me out of the corner of his eye, frowning.

"We barely managed to escape back there, and now you think we can fight them? They've already killed half my squad. We don't even know how many of them there are."

"You're right. I'm sorry. I got carried away by *The Charge of the Light Brigade.*"

"The what?"

I shake my head. "Never mind."

Dad leans on me more heavily with every step. I can feel his bones pressing against his skin. He seems old and worn down.

He doesn't complain, but his skin has gone pale, his mouth a grim line of pain. I wish I had some more pain killers to give him, but we've used them up. All we can do is grit our teeth and keep putting one foot in front of the other.

41

A distant whispering comes out of the darkness, like sunset winds flowing through the canyon. Mai stands astride the trail, blocking our way. Her voice is soft and urgent.

"The underground river is ahead. I don't think we should lead them to it."

My dad nods. "I agree. That river is too important."

"What do we do?"

He bares his teeth in a grimace.

"We have to find another way."

The cave here is soft earth, the walls fractured into hundreds of tiny crevices. Water trickles down them, monsoon rain filtering through from the surface. Some of the crevices are only centimeters wide. Others are big enough for two men to pass comfortably.

Still, none of them seem stable enough for a squad in heavy armor. Especially now that the rain has started. Nothing is stable in the monsoon. Walls that have stood for a thousand years can wash away overnight.

My mind races. "The terrain is on our side. We can move faster than they can. If we split up, we might be able to lose them."

"We might lose ourselves in the process," Mai says. "Once you leave the known routes down here, it's hard to find your way back."

"That's possible. But would you rather get lost in the dark or be cut to pieces?"

Mai and my dad exchange uneasy glances, but neither of them looks panicked. These are experienced rebels. They've been fighting this war a long time.

I close my eyes and focus, feeling in the dark for the warm sparks of the Guardians' greicagin shards. There. About a hundred meters behind us. Six of them. I focus harder, trying to get a read on their weapons. Every scrap of intel is vital at this point.

As I concentrate, something strange happens. I become aware of more than just the shards behind us. In my mind, the walls of the tunnels take shape, glowing faintly, illuminated as clear as day.

How is that possible?

The answer comes as soon as I form the question.

Dust. The dust of Greica covers everything. There are greicagin grains in the dust.

A fresh wave of adrenaline makes my heart pound.

I kneel and sketch as quickly as I can, tracing the tunnel system in the dirt. I can map the terrain. This is a serious advantage.

"New plan," I whisper. "This is the cave system surrounding us."

They squat around me, eyes intent, nodding and asking questions as I sketch.

Calling it a plan is probably too strong a word. I don't have the slightest idea what will happen once we split up. Dead ends and deadfalls lurk out there in the darkness. Collapsing walls that offer no escape.

Still, they watch me and nod their heads as if I know what I'm talking about. As if I'm not making assumptions and guesses. Guesses our lives are riding on.

If we can get the Guardians to split up, we've got a chance. Tunnel fighting is a unique challenge. Tunnels twist and turn, cutting off sight lines and communication. There's no way to coordinate down here.

The Outsiders are used to this type of fighting. They live in underground labyrinths. Superior numbers, arms, and armor don't mean much when you're alone in the dark. Still, if a Guardian catches one of us in the clear, they'll burn us down in a blink.

Of course if the Guardian don't split up, and all follow one set of tracks… Well, in that case at least the others will escape.

Finally, I sit back on my heels.

"Any questions?"

"I don't know, Theo," Dad says. "We're outclassed and out-gunned. Aren't we better off just running?"

"Did we come here to fight, or did we come here to run?"

Mai stares at me across the map. "You think it will work?"

I shrug. "No idea. But it gives us a chance to burn those dust-suckers."

Mai considers for a minute, then nods, her ear-hoops jingling.

That's when it hits me. They're looking at me. These hardened freedom fighters are staring at me, squatting down in the dust. Listening to me make plans like I know what I'm talking about. I'm half their age, yet they're still paying attention to what I have to say like I'm an old veteran.

The realization gives me pause, and a little thrill of panic crackles up my spine. Who am I to have these people's lives in my hands? I'm just a kid. I shouldn't even be here.

"It's a good plan." Mai's voice is strangely loud in the subterranean silence.

Dad hesitates, looking like he wants to object. Instead, he bites his lip and puts a hand on my shoulder.

"It is, Theo. None of us could do better. Lead us home, son."

Knott pulls me to my feet. I brush the dust from my knees and force myself to grin, trying to project a confidence I don't feel.

"What are we waiting for then? Let's go burn some Guardians."

42

The four of us melt into the darkness, taking separate tunnels. With luck, the Guardians following us will do the same.

I keep my dad with me. Mai and Knott don't need our injuries slowing them down. Maybe together we'll add up to one whole fighter.

I close my eyes and watch the Guardians hit the intersection we just left. My pulse pounds in my temples, the pressure building as I watch. Tracking them this way is strangely familiar. Red lines and dots on a map. I feel like I'm back in the Game.

They pause, examining our boot prints on the ground, trying to figure out which way we went. I hold my breath. Will they take the bait?

The moment stretches, interminable. What are they waiting for?

Finally, they start to move. Relief floods through me as they split up, following the three different trails we've left. Then my relief curdles and dies. Three of them are coming our way.

I open my eyes and let go of the map, sighing with relief as the pressure in my head recedes. We limp through the darkness as fast as we can. My leg aches and burns with every step. My arm and shoulder throb beneath my dad's weight.

I blast the walls and ceiling behind us, trying to provoke a cave-in. No luck. The clay is too sticky here, and it only falls in small chunks. The best I can hope is that one of them will turn an ankle on the debris I've loosened.

I close my eyes again to watch the little red dots moving through the maze. The pressure in my temples returns, spiking into points so sharp they make me wince. But I keep at it, fighting to maintain focus through the pain. Some of the Guardians are right on top of Mai and Knott. I wish they had ID tags, so I'd know who was who.

"Jmini, can you label the map for me?"

There is an uncharacteristically long pause before the AI responds.

"I'm not sure what you're asking, Capitan. Label the map with what?"

I curse my own stupidity. Of course he can't label the map. The map I'm looking at is in my head. Jmini can't even see it.

"Never mind."

Dad sucks in a sharp breath and leans on me so heavily I stumble. He's pale and sweating.

"Are you OK?" It's a stupid question, but I don't know what else to say.

"Fine," he wheezes. "Something shifted in my side. Maybe a rib. It feels like someone is stabbing me with rusty metal. I need to sit down a minute."

I reluctantly lower him onto a flat stone.

"Only a minute, Dad. The Guardians are getting close."

"How do you know? And how were you able to sketch that map back there?"

"It's hard to describe." I shy away from the subject, unsure what to say.

My dad looks at me expectantly, one eyebrow raised in that infuriatingly patient way that dads have. I sigh.

"Fine, I'll tell you. But we have to keep moving."

"Fair enough." He grits his teeth and allows me to pull him back to his feet.

As we wind our way through the subterranean labyrinth, I do my best to explain the way the greicagins resonate within me.

"So it started when you got that chip implanted?"

"No, I think it was always there. At least, it's been there since my time as a deep diver in the mines, even though I didn't know what it was at the time. I think it's the reason I was so good at finding greicagin deposits."

"You could feel them underground?"

"No… Yes. It's hard to describe. It wasn't so much I could feel them as I just had a hunch which way to go. Like maybe some part of me could feel them, but that part didn't have open lines of communication to my conscious mind."

My dad nods thoughtfully. "Your subconscious. There are things that happen in there we can't explain. The brain has more capabilities than we're aware of."

I shrug. "If you say so."

"I'd guess that when you had your shard implanted it boosted your natural affinity. It made what's been happening in your subconscious accessible to the front of your brain for…" He winces and groans, doubling over. His breath hisses between his teeth.

I waver, unsure what to do. Part of me wants to ransack the medkit again, try to find something, anything that can help him. Meanwhile, the part of me that's watching the Guardians get closer wants to simply throw him over my shoulder and run.

Instead I do nothing, paralyzed by the sick sense of helplessness gnawing at my guts.

Finally, the pain eases. He takes my arm and we stagger on.

"You've been given a gift, son. I suspect there are layers of this ability you still haven't uncovered. We have to take this to Tempest. Maybe she'll know how to put your capabilities to best use."

"Keep quiet now, Dad. We're getting close."

There's a small cave ahead where several crevices come together. According to my plan, this is the place we take the Guardians down.

I close my eyes and focus on my mental map, ignoring the matching flare of pain in my head. I frown at the red dots.

"Something's wrong. Mai and Knott aren't in position."

"What's happening?"

I shake my head.

"I don't know. I can't tell what they're doing, only where they are. And where they are isn't where they're supposed to be."

"Are they all right?"

"I don't know. I can't see what they're doing." I bite my lip as the pain intensifies, rusted metal sawing through my skull. I push past it, but the map starts to blur beneath a haze of pain. Finally, I'm forced to let it go. "It doesn't look good. The Guardians are too close."

"Let's go get them." My dad pulls the cannon off his shoulder, his face grim. His lips are pale with pain, jaw muscles clenching and unclenching.

"I don't think that's a good idea, Dad. You're in no shape for a fight. It's too dangerous."

"It was your plan, Theo. If it's falling apart it's your responsibility to fix it." His eyes are fever bright. "I'm not leaving good soldiers behind. We have to make this right."

I swallow and nod reluctantly. All I really want to do is get my dad to safety.

But he's right. This was my plan. If it's gone to dust, it's my responsibility.

"All right. We'll do our best."

43

A cannon blast almost takes my head off as we round the corner. I fall to the ground and roll behind a fold in the rock, my ears ringing with the sound. What's happening? I was just looking at the map in my mind a minute ago. There shouldn't be any Guardians here.

Another blast hits the wall above me, showering my helmet with debris. I guess it doesn't matter where they should be. All that matters is that they are here.

Dad is lying in the middle of the tunnel where I dropped him, wheezing and holding his side. Completely exposed.

I poke my cannon around the rock and fire a sustained burst in the general direction of our attacker, hoping it'll make them pull back for a moment. Then I launch myself into the open and grab Dad under the armpits, frantically dragging him back toward cover.

He screams as my tugging re-opens his wound, but it can't be helped. If I leave him out there, he'll be burned in seconds.

Cannon fire pounds the back of my armor, underscoring the point It knocks me off balance, and I fall on top of Dad. He moans and I curse.

A real top-notch rescue effort.

I lever myself back up and brace myself, managing to stay erect when the next blast hits me. Two seconds later we're both safely behind cover.

Dad doesn't look good. He's sweating and sucking in small, quick breaths. His face is a ghastly patchwork of purple-red and pale grey.

"Hang on, Dad. I'll get you out of here."

I close my eyes and open my mind to the greicagins. Through the spike of pain, I see there's only a single attacker pinning us down. That makes me feel better.

Not a lot better: he's still got us right where he wants us. But a little. Maybe I can handle one of them.

I fire off a blind cannon burst while I do a quick check on the others. Mai hasn't moved since the last time I looked. Not good. She's either pinned down or worse. Knott appears to be at the rendezvous point, but she's got company too. At least somebody was able to stick to the plan. We sure haven't.

I open my eyes and draw my warpknife. Cannons aren't going to solve anything against Guardian armor. We could sit here and blast each other all day. I'm going to have to get up close and personal.

I squeeze off a burst from my cannon and move. Head down, charging the Guardian's position.

The soldier ducks back behind cover when I fire, as I'd hoped, so they don't see me coming until I'm right on top of them. Their eyes widen as I round the corner, their face blue in the helmet's dim interior light. They swing their cannon up in an instinctive blocking attempt.

They might as well try to block with warm thoughts.

My warpknife doesn't even slow, cutting right through the cannon and sinking up to the hilt in the Guardian's breastplate. Blood and spit spray the inside of their visor. Then they sigh, sag, and slump to the dust at my feet.

I stare down at the corpse, feeling sick. That might have been someone I went to school with. That might have been one of my friends.

Shaking, I back away. There's no time for remorse now. They made me a killer, and now they've got to live with the results. We all do.

I sling Dad's arm over my shoulder and drag him down the tunnel.

He's not walking anymore, in fact he's barely conscious. I don't know what that says about his wound, but it can't be good.

We lean against the wall for a moment, and I suck air like a man who's never had it before.

My greicagin-sight tells me Mai and Knott still haven't moved. I don't know what to do. Mai and Knott are in trouble and my dad is hanging by a thread. My plan is a complete failure.

My head is pounding, and my first instinct is to pull the ripcord: bail out and head for the river. Run like the street rat I've always been.

But Mai and Knott might still be alive. Waiting for me to come get them. Following the plan that I created.

I can't abandon them.

I drag Dad toward the whispering of the underground river. We emerge into an arching, damp tunnel. Water drips from the ceiling, forming concentric rings on the surface of the water. The river is wide and dark, swollen by the monsoon. I lower him down by the bank and prop him up against a small pile of dirt and rocks.

"Dad, stay here. I'm going to get the others. I'll be right back, OK?"

He murmurs something unintelligible, delirious with pain.

"Jmini, do you think he'll be OK here?"

"He can't even walk, Twist. Where is he going to go?"

"But will he be OK?"

"He's not going to die in the next five minutes, if that's what you're asking. Do what you have to. He'll survive until you get back."

I grimace and leave my dad wrapped in the sound of the river, reluctantly slipping away into darkness.

Away from the murmuring water, the cave becomes utterly silent. So quiet that my heartbeat hammers like a drum in my ears. I usually love the subterranean stillness, but right now it makes my skin crawl. Anyone could be waiting out there. I try to walk quietly, but every pebble skittering beneath my boots seems impossibly loud.

According to the map in my head, Mai should be fifty meters ahead of me. I slow to a careful crouch, shuffling forward, every sense straining at the silence.

I slip out into a large cavern, broken by the jagged fingers of stalagmites. The air is cool and moist. Trickling streams fall from the tips of stalactites high above, the patter of droplets echoing in the dark.

When I close my eyes, my headache spikes again, sharper than ever. The greicagin map tells me the nearest Guardians are a hundred meters away, on the other side of the cavern. They shouldn't be able to see me from there, but they're close enough to be dangerous. I need to get in and get Mai out quickly.

The map falls away as I open my eyes, my breath sounding impossibly loud inside my visor. I creep forward, gripping my cannon so hard my fingers ache. Forty meters.

I squib the recognition code to Mai, so she doesn't take me for a Guardian and accidentally shoot me.

Mai is a dark shape resting at the base of a stalagmite three times as thick as her torso. She doesn't move, just sits there, watching me approach.

Squatting down beside her, I lift my visor.

"Are you hurt?"

There's no response, not even a slight shake of her head. Dread makes me shiver.

I don't want to shine my light on her face. But I make myself do it anyway. Maybe she's hurt or unconscious. Maybe she needs my help.

Setting my helmet light to the dimmest setting, I lean close, flicking it on. The light reveals a shattered faceplate and Mai's face, slick with blood. Her silver ear hoops sparkle. Her mouth is slack, her eyes wide and staring.

My stomach drops. I want to do something for her. Take her with me, back to whatever family she has out in the scablands. She deserves that much, at least.

But I can't.

Instead, I lay her on her back so she looks like she's sleeping. I cross her hands over her chest and gently close her eyes.

"You were a good soldier, Mai," I whisper. "You protected those who needed it. Thank you for your service. Rest now."

It's all I have time for at the moment. The living need me more.

I ball my hands into fists and bite down on my lip to keep from screaming. I taste blood, frustration and rage coursing through me. This is my fault. My stupid plan has cost three people their lives today.

"I'm sorry." I touch Mai's helmet with my gloved fingers. Warm tears wet my cheeks. "I'm so sorry."

Stark lights pop on, illuminating the ugly burn marks through the center of Mai's chest.

Rory's voice calls out. "Quite the touching scene, Twisty. You and the Outsiders. I always knew you were a traitor."

I whirl, half-blinded, squinting into the glare of the lamps. Behind the lights, three cannons are leveled at my chest.

44

"That's ironic coming from someone who sold his squad out, Rory."

I'm shaking with anger, fighting the urge to draw my warpknife and launch myself at him. But it's three against one and my dad is waiting for me. If I don't make it back, he'll bleed out in the darkness. I have to be smart.

"School isn't real life, Twisty. You're selling out all of Canyon City. How does Kass feel about that?" I don't answer, but he reads it on my face. "Oh, she doesn't know yet? I'll be sure to tell her the good news."

I scream and charge, releasing a barrage of cannon fire. The Guardians react professionally, dropping behind cover to return fire.

That instant of distraction is all I need. I veer to the side, darting between a pair of thick stalagmites. It hurts me to run away, but it's the right play today. Throwing my life away won't help anyone. You've got to pick your battles, and the battle that counts is larger than this one.

My breath rasps as I dodge and weave between the rocks, frantically trying to remember the map in my head. The downside to my greicagin sight is I have to close my eyes to use it. There's no time for that now. I've got to keep moving and pray I'm still on the right track.

A stalagmite explodes beside me, dust and debris rattling against my armor. I duck and weave, running with everything I've got. It can't end here. I just got my family back. Dad and Ianna are waiting for me.

Cannon fire punches me in the back, slamming my face into a dark wall of rock. I bounce off it and stumble, going down hard in the dust.

"Stay down, Twist," Rory yells. "I'd rather take you in alive."

Is that supposed to be comforting? He wants me alive so they can torture me. Extract every bit of information I possess about the Outsiders. Make me betray everyone I love. No thank you. I'd rather be dead.

But I'm not giving up yet.

I scramble to my feet, head down, legs pumping. The world is dust and cannon fire. Exploding against walls, pounding the back of my armor. Somehow I stay on my feet, keep moving forward.

I squeeze into a jumbled maze of stalagmites spaced less than a meter apart, slipping between them like a rockbaby. This is the place I was trying to get to. The Guardians would have to be right on top of me to see where I'm going now.

Ducking and dodging, I dance around the stalagmites. The cannon fire stops, and all I can hear is my heart hammering in my ears, my rasping breath. With any luck, I'll lose them in this labyrinth.

There's no set path through the jumble, just a direction. West. Keep heading west. Back toward the river.

I step out of the far side of the maze and freeze, listening.

"Any sign of them, Jmini?"

"Negative, Capitan."

"Good. Keep your eyes open. I need to shut mine for a minute."

I close my eyes and push past the pain in my temples, tuning in to the greicagin flow around me. Slowly, the terrain takes shape. I focus my attention forward, trying to find the river. There. Sand swirls along the river bottom like a trail of stars. I draw my attention back, tracing the path from there to here. It's not far.

Dad is lying right where I left him, slumped against the rock. Little streams of water trickle down through the porous ceiling now, turning the entire cavern into a massive shower. Dad is lying so still my heart freezes with dread, but when I kneel beside him the soft, even hiss of his breath tells me he's sleeping.

"Dad." I shake his shoulder. "Dad, wake up. We've got to go."

"What?" He jerks awake, then smiles when he sees me. "Theo."

"Mai is dead, Dad. The Guardians got her. We have to get out of here before they get us too."

His eyes go dark. "Mai is dead?"

"I'm sorry. It's my fault. I guess my plan wasn't very good. I should have listened to you. We should have run. The river is our best chance. You're sure it runs out to the scablands?"

He nods, face slack with shock. "All right, let's go."

He hisses with pain as I pull him to his feet. The rocks are round and slippery underfoot, and I have to step carefully. Dad sags against me, nearly a dead weight in my arms. Progress is painstakingly slow.

We're ten meters from the river when a cannon shot hits Dad in the back, ripping him from my grasp. We go down in a puddle, the icy water a shock against my face and neck. I come up spluttering, stumbling on the slick rocks, fighting to regain my footing.

"Give it up, Twisty." Rory's voice echoes in the dark. "We've got you dead to rights."

Chunks of wet ceiling fall as shots ricochet off my armor. The surface of the river is only a few meters away, glittering in the multicolored cannon fire like fireworks in the night. But there's no cover out here. We're dead if we don't move.

"Jmini, if I buy you some time, can you get my dad into the water?"

"I've got a ground-drone that might be able to pull his weight, but it'll be slow going."

"Launch it."

I stand and draw my warpknife.

"You want me, Rory? Why don't you come and get me? Let's settle this thing once and for all."

The cannon fire dies.

"You must think I'm an idiot." There's a sneer in Rory's voice. "We've got you outnumbered and outgunned. Why would I give that up?"

"It's all right if you're scared, Rory. I did take your hand off the last time."

Ghengis's deep laughter booms across the cavern.

Rory's warpknife blazes, a blue crescent in the darkness.

"I was going to let you live, Twist. Old times and all that. But if that's the way you want it…"

He strides forward, and I advance to meet him. Our warpknives are the only light in the cavern, blazing blue and green. The unsheathed energy makes the shard beneath my collarbone itch.

I keep my eyes fixed on Rory, resisting the urge to glance back and check on my Dad. Jmini's drone needs time to work. I have to keep the Guardians distracted as long as I can.

As Rory gets closer, I can see his face, illuminated beneath his visor. His mouth is twisted with rage.

It's hard to believe we were crew once. A couple of rockheads fighting against the spoiled Sunriser kids. Working together to win the Guardian Tournament. Us against them.

I even thought we were friends.

But that all changed when Rory sold us out to Ghengis's team during our final exam. It would have worked too, if Grab hadn't come screaming out of the storm in his wounded Hummingbird to take out Ghengis. Sacrificing himself so we could win the Game.

I never thought a kid from Sunrise would be the one to show me what it really means to be crew.

Or that a fellow rockhead would sell me out over a girl.

My heart constricts at the thought of her.

Kass is gone now. I had to give her up along with everything else. I hope my defection doesn't reflect on her too badly. I hope she can find a way to forgive me some day.

Rory's prosthetic hand gleams as he closes within striking distance. I took that hand from him during the final exam. I consider it fair payment for his betrayal of our crew.

Judging by the fury in his eyes, Rory doesn't agree with my assessment.

He comes in low, thrusting at my thigh. I parry and spin away, swiping with my backhand as I disengage. My blade draws a thin line across his chestplate.

It's not deep enough to have reached his skin, but the cut got his attention. He stops himself from making an impulsive counterattack and circles instead, caution damping down his anger.

I was lucky to goad him into this duel. Rory was the best shot in our class. With a cannon he would pick me apart. With a warpknife, up close, I've got a chance.

I watch him come to this realization as well. He lunges in again, but he's hesitant now, and I parry the thrust easily. I catch him across the forearm with a quick counterstrike, drawing the first blood of the bout.

The fury in his eyes changes to fear. He's remembering all the extra hours I put into warpknife practice. Extra hours he spent on the target range with his cannons instead. Maybe he's remembering the time I ran circles around Ghengis in dueling class; the day I first caught Kass's eye.

Or maybe he's remembering how I killed Octav right in front of him. How I sunk my warpblade through the center of his chestplate while the sandstorm raged around us.

He knows he can't back down now. He'll lose all the respect he's worked so hard to build. As a former rockhead, he'll never get that respect back.

But if he doesn't back down, I am going to kill him.

His mind is working overtime, getting in the way of his body. He stumbles over a rock. I take advantage of his distraction to open a gash across his ribs.

I'm moving in to press my advantage when a new voice rings out in the darkness.

"Stop!" A shining figure steps into the cavern. A red warpknife blazes a crescent in their fist. "This one is mine."

Rory backs away, stark relief in his eyes. The shining figure strolls forward to take his place. My blood goes cold as the face behind the visor comes into focus.

45

"I've been looking forward to this." Julius's voice sounds the same as his twin's did. Arrogant. Dismissive. Murderous.

Julius raises his warpknife high, curling it up over his head in the scorpion-like fighting stance his brother favored. A shiver runs down my spine. Octav was the best duelist in our class. If Julius is half as good, I'm in trouble.

"My sister sends her regards," I growl, sinking into a defensive crouch.

"As does my brother."

Julius lunges forward with astonishing speed, his warpknife plunging straight for the center of my chest. Caught off guard, I barely turn the blade aside, and the edge burns across my ribs.

Julius isn't messing around. He wants to end me, and to end me now.

He comes in again. Even though I'm ready this time, I still barely manage to parry his strike. I feel warm blood run down over my bicep.

He fights just like his dead twin. Memories of sparring with Octav in Merrimac flash through my mind. He used to toy with me, sinking his warpknife into my thigh over and over. Try as I might, I never could parry his blows.

Julius attacks again. This time I manage a counterstrike, scoring his armor just below the shoulder. In return, I get another slash across the ribs.

Trading blows with him is a losing strategy. He's ahead in the blood count. If we trade cut for cut, I'm done.

I've got to be better. Faster. I have to take Julius down for the Outsiders. For Ianna.

I didn't come all this way to fail here.

Launching a complicated series of feints and thrusts, I put all my skill and training to use. My breath rasps inside my helmet. Sweat trickles down my temple. I keep pressing. I've got to break through.

He defends like a dust-devil, always moving, sweeping every blow aside. His movements are so practiced, so precise, it's like we're back in the Game. I'm fighting an avatar programmed for perfection.

Julius nicks my shoulder again. Then my left thigh. I feel myself slowing down, blood loss taking its toll.

I'm not going to win this. I can't win this.

But I won't lose alone either. If I'm going down, Julius is coming with me.

Gathering myself, I prepare for a final, desperate charge. If I leave myself open, I can get through his defenses. His pretty dueling technique isn't designed to fend off a suicide charge. He'll get me, but I'll get him too.

It's fitting, really. Julius and I started down this path when we tangled during the final qualifying run for the Guardian Tournament. If I hadn't beat him then, I would have never become a Guardian, and he never would have gone into politics.

Now we've come full circle.

I crouch and gather myself. This is it.

As I spring forward, my foot slips on the wet rocks. I flail and fall sideways, my leg skidding out from under me. Somehow I keep my feet.

But my guard is down.

I feel Julius's warpknife coming and flinch away, turning my head just enough to keep him from spitting my skull like a boneworm. The edge of his blade slices across my right eye. Searing pain burns through my skull.

Screaming I fall, pressing my hand to my face. Blood runs between my fingers.

I lie on the ground, whimpering, blinded by blood and tears.

Julius kicks my warpknife away and sneers down at me.

"So it ends. I've been waiting for this day a long time."

"Stop!"

My warpknife flares back to life. My dad stumbles out of the darkness, gripping the blade in a trembling hand.

He looks like he can barely stand, but he plants himself in front of me and fixes Julius with a glare.

"Stay away from my son."

Julius's eyes widen, then the corners of his mouth twist up.

"Is this your father, Twist? How perfect. Family for family."

"Don't…"

I stretch out a bloody hand, but Julius is already in motion. The tip of his warpknife darts forward, emerging red from the center of my father's back.

Dad makes a soft, surprised sound. Like breath escaping. Then he crumples to the ground.

"Dad!" I scoot forward and wrap my arms around him. His face is white with pain and shock. I pull the sealant from my medkit, frantically spraying the ragged wound in his chest. "Don't worry, Dad. I'll get you out of here. We'll get help."

"How very optimistic of you." Julius cocks his head in mild curiosity, as if he's watching a shellbaby try to drag itself back into its burrow. "Unfortunately, this isn't one of those idiotic serials where the underdog overcomes all obstacles. The real world doesn't work that way."

A heavy burst of cannon fire lances out of the darkness, flinging Julius away. Knott's voice fills the stunned silence.

"That's what you think, rich boy. Hold onto your Dad, Twist. Things are getting messy in here."

The Guardians light up Knott's heavy armor, blue and red beams dancing in the dark. Knott's return fire goes high, missing everyone.

I have time to wonder if her AI's targeting is off ... before the ceiling comes crashing down.

46

———

I hold onto my dad as an avalanche of mud sweeps over us. I'm tumbled and spun around, rolled across the rocks like a child rolling down a hill. The mud tries to tear Dad away from me, but I grip tight, my arms straining against the pull.

Abruptly, we're underwater, so cold it takes my breath away.

Flailing I struggle to surface, unsure which way is up. My lungs burn. Just when I don't think I can hold my breath anymore, my face breaks the surface and I greedily suck air.

My feet find the bottom. We're in the river, pushed far out into the water by the force of the mudslide. Frigid water seeps in through the joints of my armor, making my feet go numb. The water flows quickly, and the rocks beneath the surface are even more slippery than the stones on the bank, forcing me to move with small, careful steps.

I grab Dad and slosh forward, slipping and falling and getting up again, trying to hurry in that dreadful slow-motion way you move through water. Dad has gone limp, floating on the surface of the river. The current keeps trying to pull him away from me. I fight it until my panicked brain finally gets the message.

"Inflate the bladders, Jmini."

Cannon fire flickers around me as I lower myself into the water.

Someone in Rory's crew has found me. I pull Dad's head up onto my chest, curling my body to keep my armor between him and the cannons as best I can. The bladders keep me buoyant, turning my armor into a raft. Now that I'm floating, the current pushes us along faster than my clumsy feet did. We've got a lower target profile too — less area for the Guardians to shoot at.

Rory's crew keep pace along the river bank, illuminating the water with their harsh white lights. The surface of the river bucks and undulates, carrying us up and down with what feels like terrifying speed. But the Guardians along the shore have no trouble pacing us, peppering my armor with a steady stream of fire. The impact of the shots rocks me, their insistent sizzling louder than the roar of the water in my ears.

Lying there is a terrible, helpless feeling. My wounded eye burns and aches. My dad might be bleeding out.

Panicking, my brain keeps urging me to get up and run, but I know that will make me move slower, not faster. All I can do is float and absorb fire, like a piece of driftwood caught in a flash flood.

Abruptly the cannons stop firing, and a startling silence rushes in to fill the void. I fight the urge to pick my head up and look around.

"Twist, can you hear me?" Rory's voice echoes off the cavern walls. He's fishing for a reaction, trying to determine if I'm still alive.

I ignore him and close my eyes, focusing in on the greicagins. I need to find Knott. Make sure she's OK.

It's nearly impossible to concentrate. I've never floated in a river before, and the feeling is terrifying. So much water sweeping me along, taking me wherever it wants. If the bladders in my armor deflate, I'll sink like a stone. I've never felt so small and helpless.

It takes all my willpower to lie still when every instinct is screaming at me to get up and run. Every muscle is clenched and tense. My wounded eye is on fire, and my head pounds like a struck nail. My fight-or-flight dial is turned all the way up. In both directions.

I struggle through it. Clench my teeth and keep my eyes closed. Breathe into it. Slowly, the red map wavers to life in my head. When it does, it's so startling I almost sit up and yelp.

The water around me is full of greicagin particles. I'm floating in a wide, glittering flow. It's the most beautiful thing I've ever seen. It takes my breath away.

With an effort, I tear myself away from the river. I have to find Knott. It looks like the mudslide has separated her from the Guardians. I see her red dot moving away from the cavern, in the opposite direction. I exhale with relief. She's on her own in hostile territory, but she's safe for now. Hopefully, she'll find her own way out.

I sink back into the sparkling red river, cradling my dad's head on my chest. I feel like we're moving through one of the planet's arteries. Carried away on a river of blood.

47

The river pulls us through the darkness for a long time, leaving Rory and Julius far behind. I don't know how long I float, blind except for the red greicagin map I see every time I close my eyes. The freezing water numbs my pounding head. One good thing, anyway.

I keep thinking about Mai and the rest of the team. All of them dead. Buried in a tunnel forever.

It's my fault. My rush to get revenge on Julius. My halfcocked plan. I should be the one who's dead, not them. It's not right I get to escape and they don't.

I float along in the first rush of the monsoon season. The one month every year when the surface runs with water. It slices down through the soft walls of the canyons and caves, reshaping as it goes. Overnight, a path you've taken for years might disappear, replaced by a raw slashing cut through a thousand-meter wall you thought would be there forever. Every year Canyon City is erased, and every year it is sculpted anew.

Maybe that's what water's real purpose is. It's not for drinking, or bathing. It's for changing things. Sweeping away the old. Revealing the new.

The tunnel around me is getting light. I can see the curve of my dad's head on my chest and make out the looming silhouettes of boulders on the bank as we sweep by. At first I think it's my imagination, but after a few minutes I realize it's really happening. The subterranean darkness has become a grey scale, lightening before my good eye by slow degrees.

My other eye is crusted over and blind. Burning and aching. I wonder how much damage Julius's warpknife did to it. I wonder if it will ever see again.

The river sweeps us out into a dim cavern. Thin shafts of light lance down through cracks in the ceiling and walls. The weak light feels like high noon to my light-starved eye, and I squint against the relative glare. The river widens, taking advantage of the space, becoming slow and shallow in the process. I stretch a cautious foot toward the bottom and discover it's only a meter deep.

I struggle to my feet and slog heavily to the shore, pulling my dad along behind me. I sink onto the pebbly bank, chilled and exhausted. I've had enough water to last the rest of my life.

Dad's face is pale, his lips tinged with blue. But he's still breathing.

"What now, Jmini? Do you know where we are?"

The cavern is long and narrow, and the streaks of weak light give it a murky glow. The bank I'm sitting on is the only land not covered by water, a rocky shelf ten paces across. As monsoon season progresses, the river will probably rise and swallow it too.

"The walls of the cave are blocking me," Jmini replies. "Try climbing to one of the cracks and see if we can get a window to the outside world."

"What about my dad?"

"I don't think he'll notice one way or another."

He's got a point. Dad is passed out, dead to the world. I don't want to leave him alone, but I'm not doing him any favors sitting here. He needs to be in a medrig, and to get him into one, I have to find a way out of here.

"I'll be right back, Dad. Hang in there." I don't think he hears me, but I feel better saying it.

The wall is cracked and jagged, easy climbing. I haul myself up to a crevice that's taller than I am and peer out, blinking in the grey monsoon light. The gloomy valley beyond tells me we're definitely outside the wall. Other than that, I haven't got a clue.

"Any luck, Jmini?"

"I'm scanning, give me a minute."

I close my eye and do some scanning of my own while I wait. Outside, the landscape glows with the same greicagin traces as the walls of the cave system. It's like when I used to have Jmini turn the world into a line-grid simulation during the Game. All clean contour lines and folds. Except now the lines are red, not blue. And I'm the one creating the simulation.

I stretch my mind, wondering how far I can push this new sense of the world. The contour lines stretch across the valley outside, and up the wall on the far side. My heart races as I follow them up and over the top of the cliff, mapping the land beyond my immediate line of sight. A sinkhole catches my attention, and I follow it down into another cave, the passages spidering out into a web of possibilities…

"Capitan. Capitan!"

Somewhere far away, Jmini is calling me. I struggle to pull myself back, reeling my consciousness in from the depths of the far-flung cave system.

"Yes?" My lips feel funny and my mouth is dry, as if it's been hanging open for a long time. Spikes of pain pound my temples.

"Finally." Jmini's voice is thick with relief. "You had me worried there for a minute."

"Worried?" My thoughts are sluggish inside my skull. I rub my hands over my face in an effort to get them moving. "Why would you be worried?"

"You've been staring into space for ten minutes, oblivious to my attempts to talk to you. I was starting to wonder if we'd lost you for good."

I swallow, trying to work saliva down into my dry throat.

"Sorry. I was mapping the outside in my mind. I guess I got lost."

"Perhaps you should spend less time in your imaginary realm. It's not as if we have all the time in the world. Your father is still waiting for you."

That snaps me back to full alert. "Oh spines."

I rush back down to the pebbly beach, my heart in my throat. Dad is still lying where I left him, pale and still. I can't see his chest moving. I put my ear to his lips, and for a panicked moment I think I've lost him. Then I feel the faintest breath tickling my skin. Relief surges through me, and I sag down onto the rocks.

"Thank the dust devils."

Jmini clears his throat. "Well, now that we've got that out of the way, would you care to hear what I found out?"

"Found out about what?"

"About the outside world. Where we are. You know, the reason we climbed up to that crevice in the first place."

"Oh, right. Yes." I sit up and try to look attentive. Can Jmini even see my face? Never mind, that's a question for another time. "What did you find out?"

"As far as I can determine, the Outsiders have been wiped out."

"What?" I'm on my feet now, anxious to go somewhere. But I don't know where to go. "What do you mean, wiped out?"

"I mean that the base we were in this morning has been reduced to rubble, along with a number of other locations. I see no sign of Outsider activity."

"That's got to be a mistake. Ianna was in that base. They've just gone underground again." I stammer, my breath hitching in my throat. Ianna can't have gotten free only to die the next day. It can't be true.

"Possibly, but I would expect to see signs if that were the case. My drones don't see anything but dust and rocks. I'm sorry, Twist."

I'm sitting down on the rocks again, my head spinning. There's a pain in my chest like someone's stuck a warpknife through me. I can't breathe.

Beside me, my dad jerks and a horrible, rattling sound bubbles up from somewhere deep within. All my hair stands on end, and a chill shivers my body. The rattle goes on for what feels like forever, then it cuts off abruptly, taking the last of my dad's breath with it.

Grief rips through me, painful sobs tearing out my insides. I cry like I never have before. I cry for my dad. I cry for my sister. I cry for Mai, and my mother, and every other mother in Canyon City. Every single person whose children are born into this awful dust.

I sob and I wail and I weep.

Eventually, I run out of tears. I sit dazed and numb. Staring at my dad's body. Staring at the water flowing past. Staring into the darkness.

I feel like I'm part of the stone. Part of the dust.

I don't notice the daylight fading, or the cavern darkening around me. I don't notice the walls taking on a red glow, or the water sparkling beside me. I don't notice that I'm seeing the greicagin glow with my eye open or think about how strange that is.

I sit there for hours. Not moving. Not thinking. Utterly hollowed out and empty. Alone in the red not-darkness.

A sound draws my attention. A massive Rock Horror strides up the river, its sharp feet slicing through the current, making barely a splash as it steps. On its back sits a man. Beneath his ragged cloak, his eyes shine with a metallic sheen.

"Come on, boy. It's time to go."

Rust extends his hand.

I stare at it like I've never seen a hand before, like a newborn in the face of an incomprehensible world. Rust just sits there, waiting. After a long time, I reach up and take his offered hand.

Rust pulls me up onto the Horror behind him. Its carapace is cool and smooth under my fingers, solid beneath my legs. It lurches into motion.

We crawl away into red darkness, carried by the sound of water and the clicking steps of a Horror.

END

***

I know, I know. Cliffhangers suck. I apologize. But don't worry! You don't have to wait long to find out what happens next. PEAK, Book Three of The Crimson Dust Cycle, comes out May 18th! You can pre-order it now and get it as soon as it drops. Pre-order available at www.arquinworlds.com

Also, while I've got your attention, I'd just like to mention that reviews are super-important! We all look at what others have to say before trying something new, it's just human nature. So if you enjoyed SLIDE, please take a moment to write a review, so that others can find this story and enjoy it as well. This handy universal link will take you to most online booksellers: https://books2read.com/u/banoL2

Thank you!

ABOUT THE AUTHOR

J.S. Arquin lives in his own worlds. At least, that's what his teachers always told him when they caught him reading books inside his desk instead of paying attention in class.

These days, he fills those worlds with stories of fantastic places & extraordinary people, which he dutifully shares with his readers. He still lives inside them. He is aware that some people claim there is a "real world" out there.

J.S. remains unconvinced.

When not writing, he spends his time narrating audiobooks, working on his podcast, The Overcast, drinking too much caffeine, playing board games and ping pong, and riding his bicycle in the rain.

He is hard at work on the next book in the Crimson Dust Cycle.

Explore his worlds and sign up for his exclusive reader group at www.arquinworlds.com

****

Found a typo? This book has been through several rounds of editing and proofing, but mistakes happen. Please inform us of any errors you find so that we can fix them for the next edition. email: js@arquinworlds.com

twitter.com/JS_Arquin

ALSO BY J.S. ARQUIN

TWIST: A Crimson Dust Cycle Prequel

ASCENT: Book One of the Crimson Dust Cycle

SLIDE: Book Two of The Crimson Dust Cycle

And Coming May 18th, 2020:

PEAK: Book Three of The Crimson Dust Cycle